OTTERS IN SPACE:

THE SEARCH FOR CAT

HAVANA

by Mary E. Lowd

Otters In Space: The Search for Cat Havana

Copyright © Mary E. Lowd
2012

Cover Artwork by Doc Marcus
http://www.furaffinity.net/user/docmarcus

Published by FurPlanet Productions
Dallas, Texas
www.furplanet.com

ISBN 978-1-61450-043-8

Printed in the United States of America
Second Edition Trade Paperback 2012

Table of Contents

Acknowledgements

For my husband, my mother, and my sister.

With special thanks to Felicia Day, Peter Watts, Ryan North, and Adam Young for The Guild, Blindsight, Dinosaur Comics, and Owl City, *respectively.*

Chapter 1

The bus stop sign and shelter were in front of a giant, white church. The Church of the First Race was an historical building, preserved from the time when humans still walked the Earth. It dwarfed the taller but smaller-scale high-rises around it. It was the oldest building in New LA. Kipper had been inside once and sat on the monstrous pews, but, like most cats, she didn't feel comfortable with First Race doctrine. It was a dog religion—they preached that humans, the First Race, had left Earth as emissaries to the stars and would return to bring all the peoples of Earth into a confederation of interstellar sentience. Someday.

Maybe that's why the dogs hadn't developed space travel themselves yet. They had an amusement park on the moon, but they had to borrow otter technology to put it there and lease otter technology to keep it running. That's right, the otters surprised everyone and were the second race to make it off of their native rock. Except, unlike humans, they didn't just disappear. They filled the skies with space stations and space ships. By all accounts, they liked it better up there. Kipper wondered if she'd like it better up there too.

But cats don't go into space. They live in the inner cities, working low-paying jobs, and the dogs like it that way. A poor cat is a controlled cat, but now that the average cat income was increasing for the first time since cats won the right to vote, dogs were getting scared.

As Kipper looked around her, she twitched the tip of her tail nervously. There were three cats waiting at the bus stop, in addition to her and her sister Petra. And one Chihuahua on a cell phone.

Petra was an orange tabby, and she had the erratic temper to match her coloring. Sometimes Kipper was jealous of Petra's brightly colored stripes, as she, herself, was the most common of all kinds of cats. A plain gray tabby. Petra's bold coloring came with a bold personality, as if the bright, angry color of her fur branded Petra down to her very soul. Sometimes Kipper was jealous of that too. Yet, it came with a price. Petra could be unpredictable. Uncontrollable. Even for herself.

"How did I get myself into this?" Petra asked Kipper, barely loud enough for the words to whisper past her whiskers.

Before Kipper could answer with the long story of how Petra and their brother Alistair had stayed up late, drinking spiked cream and egging each other on, challenging each other with greater and greater outrage over the *system*...

"I guess I'd best get on with it," Petra said. The moment of lucid uncertainty gone, Petra stepped closer to the bus stop. She stared at each of the cats in turn, trying to catch the eyes of their fellow commuters. The tabby in the rain slicker flattened his ears; the fat Jellicle on the bench gave her a blank stare; and, the other tabby simply looked away. The Chihuahua smiled with friendly, sparkly eyes. Petra probably could have struck up a conversation with him if he weren't on the phone. Maybe the other cats would have listened in.

Since that wasn't an option, Petra drew a deep breath between her teeth and set her eyes on the Jellicle. Kipper watched in awe as Petra stalked straight up to him, sat her fiery orange self down on the bench beside his black and white splotched girth, and said, "My name's Petra Brighton, and I'm running for district representative."

Petra stuck out her paw and the Jellicle stared at it dumbly. "Don't you think it's time we had more cats in the government?" Petra said.

The Jellicle's eyes widened and darted to either side. He clearly felt put on the spot. Kipper could sympathize. She felt equally embarrassed watching the situation. No one likes a politician. But if *some* cat didn't do the job, all cats would pay the price... At least, that's what Petra and Alistair kept telling her.

"There's that one Abyssinian bloke," the Jellicle finally hazarded, clearly hoping Petra would go away. "Isn't he a senator?"

"Senator Adinew," Kipper offered.

"Yes," Petra said. "Adinew's doing good work. But, surely, one senator out of forty-six is hardly representative of California's feline population..." Petra raised her voice, speaking more loudly than sounded natural. It was terribly embarrassing, but, clearly, she was hoping to catch the other cats' attention. Kipper was deeply glad that she hadn't let Alistair talk her into being the figurehead for Petra. If Petra wanted to change the government, let her do it herself.

"Here in the central district, especially," Petra semi-shouted, "we cats outnumber dogs nearly four to one, but twice as many dogs vote as cats in every single election. Did you realize that?"

The Jellicle cat shook his head, and the tabby in the rain slicker kept shooting them furtive glances. He looked annoyed, but Kipper supposed that, inelegant as Petra's methods might be, she was getting her message across. It was good that the other cats were listening.

Petra had launched into her campaign speech full throttle by now: "Cats have been gaining power and influence in this country and the world like never before. There are multi-billionaire cats and cats with important jobs in internationally valuable companies." Petra stood up and held her paws out in a gesture of decisiveness. "But we don't have sufficient representation in government to protect the ground we're gaining."

Kipper could see the bus approaching out of the corner of her eye and realized she was relieved. She was happy that Petra was being heard, but it was hard to be too happy. This would all keep getting worse as the campaign went on.

The bus was a block away now, and Petra must have seen it too. She started wrapping her speech up. "If we don't stand up for our rights," she said, a stridency in her voice that grated against Kipper's ears, "then the dogs are going to lock us down worse than we ever had it before feline suffrage. The right to vote doesn't mean a thing unless you *use* it. Here..." Petra started rifling through her bag, but Kipper had already taken the fliers out. She held them out to Petra who took them as the bus pulled up to the curve, splashing muddy

3

water on the tabby's rain slicker. The Jellicle waddled his way off the bench, looking more than a little relieved.

"Have a flier," Petra said, pushing a cheap photocopy toward the Jellicle who was much too large to become invisible, and clearly regretted that. "It'll tell you all about the laws the dogs are trying to slide under our whiskers this election. Here, you too..."

Petra pawned off fliers to each of the three reluctant cats. The Chihuahua reached out a paw to accept one too, but he took his eagerly. The cell phone was still pressed into his pointed, catlike ear, and Kipper wondered if he'd been listening or if he thought it was the flier for a rock band.

"That went pretty well," Petra said, falling in next to Kipper.

"Sure," Kipper said, unenthusiastically. But when she looked over at her sister, she could see that Petra's fur was slightly fluffed. "It went fine," she said, bumping her shoulder against Petra's as they boarded the bus. "Even that dog wanted your flier."

On the bus, Petra was clearly sizing up the situation. She'd been speaking quite loudly in her conversation with the Jellicle, but Kipper didn't think it would be enough for Petra to make herself heard on the bus. There were too many black labs jocularly arguing over last night's scramball scores. Kipper was relieved when Petra relaxed into her seat. Hopefully that would be the end of her campaigning until after work.

Kipper supported her sister's decision to run for office one hundred percent, but, honestly, thinking about political issues made her head spin. It made her tired, and she didn't want to hear about it anymore.

For the first time ever, a few cats could afford the prohibitively expensive cost of a trip into space and a stay at Moonville Funpark. Kipper wasn't one of them. In fact, the number of cats who could was practically countable on Kipper's claws. It was small, but it was symbolic. And the dogs were worried. So, Senator Morrison—a fundamentalist, right-wing Sheltie with an inferiority complex— had proposed a new law banning cats from space travel.

To Petra's infuriation and Kipper's disappointment, the bill was working its way, against little resistance, through the legislature. There simply weren't enough cats in the government to oppose it.

And, worse, most cats didn't seem to care. Petra, on the other paw, was incensed; she and Kipper had dreamed about saving up their money and visiting the otter space stations among the stars since kittenhood. If Senator Morrison's law passed, it would be the end of that dream.

Kipper couldn't understand the other cats' attitudes. As Petra was always saying, "Sure, dogs are too doggarned busy worshipping humans to make it into space, but what's our people's excuse?" Kipper had to wonder: what would happen if cats started building space-stations of their own? Making alliances with the otters? Who knew what wonderful havoc they could wreak? No wonder dogs like Senator Morrison were scared.

With two stops to go, Kipper overheard something that made her perk up her ears and turn the left one toward the pair of cats in the seat behind her.

"I'm telling you," a silky voice said, "cats will never be equals on this world."

Kipper was glad that Petra didn't seem to hear. She looked across the bus and managed to catch sight of the speaker's reflection in the opposite window: it was a svelte, well-dressed, champagne colored Burmese.

"What're you saying?" the Burmese's seat-mate said. "We should just resign ourselves to being second-class citizens?" Kipper guessed the Burmese's friend was a Tonkinese, but it was hard to tell from the ghostly window-glass reflection.

"I'm saying we should get out of here. There's a place..." The Burmese looked around her, ears turning in all directions, and her voice lowered. Kipper strained to hear the whispered words, but it was no use. One of the black labs had started singing a scramball chant, bobbing his floppy-eared head in time. Soon, he had several rows of dogs chanting with him. When they got up and started dancing, the bulldog bus-driver had to shout at them. "Back in your seats!" he bellowed.

Petra was bristling beside Kipper. Another moment, and Petra might have been the one yelling at the dogs, rather than the bus-driver. Thank goodness for good bus-drivers.

Usually Kipper would have been annoyed by the dogs' noisy

antics too, but she was still thinking about what she'd overheard the Burmese cat say. Where did the Burmese think cats could go that wasn't on this world? The otters' space-stations? Without changing the laws down here, would cats be anything more than refugees up there? If so, would it be better being second-class citizens to *water*dogs rather than normal ones? Kipper didn't have time to continue pondering these questions: the bus was at her stop.

The Chihuahua, no longer on his cell phone, got off of the bus ahead of Petra and Kipper. He was talking to a big, ol' Chow, and the two of them were looking at Petra's flier. The folds of fur around the Chow's face made him look angry to Kipper, but Chows always looked angry to Kipper. She knew she wasn't good at reading dogs' emotions.

As the bus pulled away, Kipper saw the Chihuahua pointing Petra out to the Chow. The Chow looked Petra up and down, and then Kipper. Unless Kipper was seriously deceiving herself, he was glaring at her. She smiled up at him; his height and bulk was intimidating. There were a lot of other dogs and cats around, but none of them looked like they would interfere if the Chow wanted to cause trouble.

"You the cats with this flier?" he barked.

Kipper nodded, trying her best to look demure, but Petra's temper was flaring. "Absolutely," she intoned. "What of it?"

The Chow sniffed. "Cats got no business in government," he said, gruffly.

Arguing with dogs is a lost cause, but, even though she knew it was a mistake, Kipper couldn't hold her tongue. She had to defend her sister. "Cats have as much right to run for office as you have," she said.

The Chow didn't reply, but his eyes became narrowed slits. The Chihuahua was bouncing from one paw to the other, nervously adding distance between him and the impending disturbance. But, if Kipper and the Chihuahua thought *Kipper* was bucking for a pounding, they had no idea what inflammatory words Petra had balanced on the tip of her tongue.

"No, no, Kipper. He's right," she said. "These dogs have messed the government up so badly, they don't *deserve* our help."

Other dogs and cats began to gather around watching.

"But," Petra concluded, narrowing her eyes back at the Chow, "I'm willing to overlook that."

Kipper eyed the situation—all the fuming dogs and the crazed looking Chow especially. She realized she was watching a mob form, and Petra's performance might earn worse than a mere beating.

Well, if they were on a stage, that wasn't the performance Kipper wanted to put on. She hastily looked over the area available to her. Usually, she and Petra would walk down two blocks and then over three more to Luna Tech Industries. However, the alley behind them would work too, and it was littered with discarded cans and broken bottles. Petra might not be able to dodge a Chow's fisted paw, but Kipper was pretty sure she could dodge thrown cans and bottles.

So, she changed the rules of the game.

Making sure she had enough distance between her and the gathering mob, Kipper crouched down in the alley and picked a mostly unbroken bottle. She thought about what she was about to do, and she could feel the adrenaline start coursing through her body. It made her shaky, but she stood up, holding the green glass bottle anyway.

"Hey, dog!" she yelled. All of the dogs and most of the cats turned to look at her, but it was the Chow's mean gaze Kipper returned. Her resolve almost wilted under the Chow's angry look, but she held firm, shouting the best taunt she could think up. "Be glad it's my sister running for office, not me—if I was in government, I'd make dogs like you wear leashes!"

The Chow growled, deep in his throat, but a couple of the other dogs laughed and a few cats applauded. Oddly, the Chihuahua was among them. Kipper couldn't appreciate the success of her quip for long, though. The Chow was heading toward her. It was time to introduce the new rules of the game.

Kipper flung the green glass bottle. It arched smoothly through the air, twisting as it flew, and landed two feet in front of the Chow. Shards of glass flew at him, but he was unharmed. And disturbingly unfazed.

Kipper took a step backward, watching the Chow to see if he'd follow her lead and pick up a bottle. He snarled, but Kipper rejoiced as he leaned down to pick up a second bottle from among the debris in the alley. Kipper caught her sister's eye and jerked her head to the side, hoping Petra would understand and get the hell out of there. Whether she did or not, it was time for Kipper to make a run for it. The Chow had chosen a ragged bottle and was hefting it, feeling its weight, preparing to fling it at her.

Kipper ducked as the bottle flew past her. Its glass smashed on the pavement behind her. The shattering sound was like fireworks in her ears. While the Chow groped for another bottle, Kipper made her escape. She pivoted around, dropped to all fours, and hastily loped away. Glass broke again as she ran, and her ears flattened from the sudden sound. Worse, the shards bounced over the damp sidewalk, creating a minefield that stung the pads of her running feet.

Chapter 2

Three blocks through the alleys was farther than the Chow cared to follow Kipper throwing bottles. So, Kipper was able to emerge onto the main street and limp the last two blocks to Luna Tech. She wasn't bleeding, but her paw pads were filled with slivers. Before entering the Luna Tech lobby, Kipper leaned against the outside of the building and took a moment to carefully dig the glass shards out of her paws. As she was working, Petra came around the block and sauntered over to stand beside her injured sister.

"Nice line," Petra said. "Dogs on leashes. I especially like the way that I can either take credit for it, as your sister, or disown you as a troubled radical who I'm unfortunately related to... Depending on who asks."

"Glad you liked it," Kipper said, gingerly trying her paw on the ground.

"Absolutely. I think I won several votes." Petra opened the glass Luna Tech door for Kipper and beckoned in. Kipper tried putting weight on her paw and found the hard pavement too merciless to be borne. She limped inside. The soft lobby carpet was a huge relief.

"We should try that every day," Petra said, following Kipper inside. "Pick a scary looking dog on the bus; egg him into throwing bottles at you..."

Kipper flattened her ears and grimaced. She'd been defending Petra since they were kittens. Somehow, she'd thought the fisticuffs would end when they grew up, but, nonetheless, here she was fighting

Petra's fights all over again.

"Look, I'm gonna go on up," Petra said, ignoring Kipper's unhappiness. "You probably have to check in with Corrie..." Petra gestured toward the miniature poodle at the front desk.

"Right." Kipper had temped at Luna Tech before, but they always made her check in at the front desk and then wait to be escorted to her position. Kipper hated temping, but there weren't a lot of jobs that cats like her could get. Petra was lucky—her job wasn't much, but it was *her* job—and, Kipper always felt lucky when she got to temp near her.

Kipper approached the front desk. The miniature poodle manning it wasn't much larger than Kipper, and her white curls were long and shapeless, completely unshorn. But their cascading effect could have made a pro-scramball player fumble a free throw. Even Kipper, a cat, could see that.

"Hi," Kipper said, "I'm the temp for the accounting department." Kipper glanced at the elevator she'd be taking in a moment and noticed the security guard there. She'd seen him before, but she hadn't remembered that he was a Chow. It made her heart race. Petra didn't seem bothered, but Kipper found herself relieved to hear Corrie summoning the personnel coordinator over the intercom.

It rankled Kipper's independent nature, but the best protection from a big dog is another big dog. And the personnel coordinator, Cheryl, was a giant Golden. Kipper couldn't help but feel safe in her easy presence. Even with her mild history of conflict with dog co-workers, Kipper had never had trouble with Cheryl.

Once Cheryl ran Kipper through the basics of the specific job she'd be temping, Cheryl took her to the desk she'd be working at. Kipper was glad to find it only a few desks over from Petra's. Kipper dipped her ears salutatorily, and Petra rolled her eyes back.

"You'll report to Sahalie, as usual," Cheryl said, gesturing to the half-open door behind her.

"Right," Kipper agreed, sitting down at the desk. It was still covered with her antecedent's personal affects: several photographs, all of purebred Siamese; a hairbrush; what looked like a lucky pen; and an African violet that had been watered recently. "What happened to the cat I'm replacing?" Kipper asked.

"Violet?" Cheryl shrugged. "No one knows. She didn't show up for work on Monday, and we haven't heard from her since. Is there anything else you need?"

"No..." Kipper answered, setting down a pawful of Petra's fliers on the desk. It was strange, but this was the fifth cat she'd temped for at Luna Tech in the last year. If they had quit or called in sick, that would be one thing, but each of these five cats had simply stopped showing up. She wondered what kept happening to them. Why wasn't anyone worried about all these disappearing cats?

Fortunately, Cheryl didn't notice Kipper's concern. She was turning her head to look at the campaign fliers, which were upside down from her perspective, on the desk; she pawed them around until they were angled so she could read them. "Our Petra's running for district representative?" The soft black lining in her mouth showed when she laughed. Laughter was better than revulsion, but Kipper still didn't like it.

Clearly, Petra didn't like it either. "Is there something wrong with that?" Petra asked, stalking over with her shoulders squared, looking at Cheryl with all the cat-dignity she could summon.

"No..." Cheryl shoved the fliers back, her eyes darting back and forth between the two sisters. Having recomposed herself, she looked as if she was deciding whether to give Petra and Kipper an important piece of advice. Both cats were infuriated by her final decision: "Of course, if you're running for office," she said, "shouldn't you dye your fur?"

Kipper could feel the tip of her tail itching to twitch, and, from Petra's face, she could see that her sister was torn between feeling insulted by Cheryl or pity for her. "What's wrong with Petra's fur?" Kipper asked.

Cheryl looked the two sisters over, Petra with her flaming orange stripes and Kipper with her subdued gray. Two plain tabbies. "Well," Cheryl said, "most of the cats I can think of in government look Siamese."

It was such a dog thing to say. Only the lowest-class, trashiest cats dyed their fur to pretend they were a purer breed. Petra replied, "There's not a cat in the world, Cheryl, that can't tell the difference between a bottle-job Siamese and a real one."

Cheryl looked surprised, as if it hadn't occurred to her that cats could tell each other apart at all. "What about the blind cats?"

With great forbearance, Kipper told the Golden what any cat would know. "They could hear the difference in the timbre of Petra's voice. She'd sound like a tabby."

Cheryl shrugged as if to say, "Have it your way," or "Cats are so complicated," and left Kipper and Petra to themselves.

"First Race!" Petra exclaimed. "I *wish* it was that simple. Put on a Siamese costume, and win the election."

Kipper wondered if Petra really believed in the First Race or if she'd just picked up the expression. It was the rare cat that fell for such ridiculous dog dogmas, though it did happen. It was possible that Petra thought affecting such idiotic doggish beliefs would help her in the polls... She wanted to ask Petra about it, but she knew Petra wouldn't tell her if it was a ruse anyway. So, all she said was, "I don't think it's that easy even for a Siamese. Only a dog would think that being the right breed makes the world open up for you like a clam, gleaming with pearls inside."

"Right," Petra agreed. "Though..." She traced an extended claw along the edge of a photograph on Kipper's temporary desk—a photograph of a Siamese tom. "She's right that it would help me win the election. Anyway, I better get back to work. If I don't win, I'm still going to need this job."

Kipper kept staring at the photograph even after Petra's claw was gone. Eventually, picking it up to look at it closer. Now there was a cat who was Siamese to the bone: clear blue, almond shaped eyes; a long, triangular face with a broad nose; and huge, wide-spaced ears. *Goodness*, he was handsome. Either a brother, husband, or son of the cat whose desk he was on. And blue-blooded down to the marrow. In fact, based on the other pictures—all of them Siamese—it was a safe bet that Violet, the name on the tacky little nameplate, was as purebred as they came. Yet, she'd worked *here*, in this tiny, fishbowl of a desk in inner-city New LA.

Even Siamese cats don't have it so good. She was an *assistant* to an *accountant*. Not much of a job. Though, Kipper supposed it was a step up from *temp for* an assistant to an accountant. The fur on Kipper's neck bristled as she admitted that to herself. It really was a dog's world.

As Kipper put back the photograph, the cardboard backing slid out of the frame. A piece of paper had been folded inside, and it fell, halfway open, on the desktop. Kipper glanced around to see if she was being watched, feeling strangely embarrassed to be messing with Violet's things. But no one was looking, so she unfolded the piece of paper the rest of the way rather than simply tucking it back in the photograph.

It looked like a printout of an airline receipt—there was a confirmation code, large and boxed, at the top of the page and an overly itemized itinerary, followed by pricing information filling out the rest of the sheet. Kipper flattened the page out to examine it more closely, and she was astonished by what she found.

Kipper powered up the computer on Violet's desk and ran a few numbers through the company database. Yes, the number on the hidden paper *was* for a company credit card. Kipper was holding the receipt for a one-way ticket to Ecuador on a flight last Saturday, bought with *Luna Tech* funds.

Even stranger, there were cryptic notes scribbled at the bottom of the page. "@ SE, ask for Chip—night flight—DSA, red 1/4— Larson w/the *Manta Ray*" and so on. Kipper couldn't make out what they meant, but she knew this was the key to Violet's disappearance. Pride swelled in her chest, realizing what Violet had done...

Violet hadn't just vanished—she'd stuck it to the Dog and got *away*. Was that what the Burmese cat meant? Was there a hidden colony of cats, living free from canine rule, in Ecuador? Some sort of cat haven?

Kipper was getting ahead of herself.

Violet probably had family in Ecuador, and there was a sudden family emergency. Or maybe she decided to give up New LA and return to the place she grew up... And rejoin her extended family who ran a commune of cats living peacefully together...

In a cat haven.

Yeah, Kipper really needed to get to work. She tried to clear her mind of visions of dancing felines, far away from dog rule, and focus on the credit report Violet had been preparing before her sudden departure.

Rows and columns of numbers. Valid and invalid uses of company credit cards. The more Kipper worked with Violet's credit report, the more she started to worry about the fact that Violet had used company credit. Sure, she wanted Violet to make it down to Ecuador and be with her dying grandmother for her last days... Or dancing in a cat commune with a handsome Siamese. But, she didn't want to get in trouble herself. And, being a party to another cat's embezzlement... Well, it didn't seem like a good idea.

Kipper made herself keep working, quietly, diligently, until the morning break. Then, she found Petra in the break room and showed her the strange discovery. She even told Petra her strange, fantastical theory about a cat haven down in Ecuador. Though, from the way Petra's eyes lit up, with the crazy light that got into them sometimes, Kipper immediately regretted it.

Petra grabbed the sheet from Kipper's paws before Kipper could stop her. "I don't know if you want to get involved in this..." Kipper started to say, but Petra had already run the sheet through the copier. A fresh, warm, inky copy spat itself into the out tray. Petra picked that up too and handed the original back to Kipper, staring open mouthed and scruffy-furred back at her.

"You should take that to Sahalie," Petra said, pointing to the original she'd returned to Kipper's paws. "She's the head accountant. That way you're covered if anyone finds out Violet was stealing."

"What about you?" Kipper asked, indicating the copy. "You're the one running for office."

"So? No one knows I have a copy, and there won't be any record of a few handmade scribbles in the computers. Besides, it's not my job to keep track of what Violet was doing." Petra looked at Kipper meaningfully, clearly to say that the job of double-checking Violet's records was *hers*. "Now... SE... SE... What could that stand for?"

Kipper watched Petra mutter to herself, ears back in concentration and eyes fixed on the paper. She was torn between joining in at breaking the code and remonstrating with her sister further. How did Petra think she was going to make it in City Hall if she took stupid risks like this? Maybe it wasn't her job to keep track of whether Violet was embezzling, but there was something stranger than mere embezzlement going on. Whatever it was, it made Kipper twitchy.

Kipper shifted uncomfortably, and for a moment she thought Petra caught her drift. Petra looked up, but she didn't look at Kipper. Her eyes locked behind Kipper, and Kipper had to turn around to see what she was looking at.

To Kipper's dismay, it was the stocky but lean, medium-sized mutt named Lucky. He explained his name, when anyone asked— and sometimes when they didn't—by saying his parents were devout First-Racers and very traditional. Kipper still found it hard to believe any dog mother would name one of her new puppies *Lucky.*

Cats with names like "Stripes" or "Mouser" were much less surprising. In fact, Petra's original name had been "Marmalade," but, like most cats named by overworked, tired, and tasteless social workers, Petra had had the good sense to change her name when she came of age. Of course, some cattery orphans were luckier in their names than others. Kipper, for instance, had kept hers. She thought it was cute and ironic to be named after a fish snack. Kind of like naming a kitten Robin—the name she'd picked out for one of her own kittens some day. If she ever had any.

"What's that?" Lucky asked Petra, pointing right at the incriminating photo-copy.

Kipper was trying to come up with a line of damage control, when Petra replied flippantly, "Plans for taking over the presidency."

"Oh, yeah?" Lucky asked, grinning a wolfish, tongue-lolling grin. "Save me a seat on your cabinet when you get elected."

"Try *in* a cabinet," Petra snapped back. Then she noticed Kipper and said, "You're still here? You need to get that to Sahalie. Now, shoo!"

Kipper was loathe to leave Petra alone with Lucky, but if Petra didn't want her there, she knew there wasn't really anything she could do. She could still hear the two of them jabbing at each other, Lucky calling Petra "Mother Hubbard," as she walked down the hall.

Kipper stopped in front of the door to Sahalie's office and drew a deep breath. Whatever the receipt was about, she knew better than to make herself a party to embezzlement. Even so, she was pretty sure she could claim ignorance of cryptic, scribbled notes. So, at the last moment, she tore off the bottom half of the page and stuck it in her vest's inner pocket. Then, she ventured into the head accounting office for all of Luna Tech. The mere idea of a cat holding a position so high gave her shivers. And when she saw Sahalie, the sight of her made Kipper shiver too.

Here was a cat that could dye her fur and pass for Siamese. Everything about her was pure and pedigreed from her cavernous ears and broad nose down to her darkened toes. Everything except for the stripes, that is. At a superficial level, Sahalie looked just like Kipper. At least, a dog might think so. Any cat would know that Sahalie must be half Siamese.

"I'm glad you brought this to me." Sahalie said after Kipper showed her the document. Her voice purred as she spoke. Her stripes may have, technically, made her a plain gray tabby, but she carried herself like an Egyptian queen. Sahalie rose from her desk and closed the door to her office behind Kipper. "Have you shown this to anyone else?" Sahalie ran an extended claw along the torn edge of the sheet, gently removing it from Kipper's willing hand.

"I brought it straight to you," Kipper lied, hoping Petra would keep the lie safe. More for Petra's sake than her own.

"Straight to me?" Sahalie repeated, blinking her blue eyes. She looked surprised, but eyes like that always look surprised. "Well, good. There are some things that are better kept between *us cats.*"

"You knew about it?" Kipper asked, somehow hearing that inside Sahalie's tone. But, then, those blue eyes narrowed at her, and Kipper realized the implications of what she'd just said. "I'm sorry. I didn't mean to imply... I don't think you're..." She couldn't bring herself to say the word *embezzling.*

Sahalie flicked her ears and smiled. "It's all right," she said. "I just meant that dogs don't understand the kind of pressure a cat feels living in this society, and we need to support one another."

Kipper wondered if Sahalie meant what she was saying or if she was mocking her with quotes from Petra's fliers. Nonetheless, she decided to take a chance and ventured, "I've noticed... I've noticed this office has trouble holding on to cats."

Sahalie's wide eyes grew wider. "Do you think there's a reason they keep disappearing?"

Kipper was momentarily troubled by Sahalie's use of the word *disappearing.* But, the feeling was drowned out by her memory of Petra and Lucky squabbling. The sound of them was still ringing in Kipper's ears. "Could the dogs here be threatening cats? Antagonizing them? Somehow, subtly, forcing them to leave..."

"Well," Sahalie said, "I've never had any trouble with the dogs in this office."

Kipper could well believe it. A cat like Sahalie wouldn't stand for anything less than the best treatment. From cats, dogs, or otherwise.

"But, I'm sure it's harder for the other cats..." Sahalie's voice turned solicitous. "Have you had any trouble?"

"I'm never here more than a week or two at a time." She figured it was better not to bring her sister into this. "None of the other cats—let alone the dogs—really get a chance to interact with me."

Sahalie smiled with her eyes and put a paw reassuringly on Kipper's shoulder. Well, partly reassuringly—the other part was a light pressure toward the door. "I'll look into it, okay?" She reopened the office door, and Kipper found herself being moved outside.

"You'll let me know if you find anything?" Kipper asked, feeling the folded, torn paper in her pocket.

"Sure," Sahalie said. "But, if I were you," Sahalie turned her ears, listening in to the dogs talking by the water cooler, "I'd be a little less worried about these cats you didn't know, and a little more worried about the cat you *do* know—*your sister.*"

Kipper gulped, realizing that Petra was among the dogs, brandishing fliers at them.

"Best of luck," Sahalie wished her. "She'll have my vote." The thought was hardly reassuring. Worse, Kipper suspected Sahalie of being insincere. It would be hard to win this election if Petra couldn't even get other cats to vote for her.

She'd probably have better luck if she stopped hanging around the water cooler, yapping with the under-dogs. Or any dogs. They weren't her target demographic. Though, with the disappearing cats of Luna Tech, around here her target demographic was in short supply...

"Hey, Petra," Kipper said, taking her sister by the arm, leading her away from the water cooler. "I talked to Sahalie."

Petra was still looking back at the dogs around the cooler, even

17

though she was walking with Kipper. "I'd take that bet!" she yelled back to them. Then, finally acknowledging Kipper, "What were you saying?" But, instead of waiting for Kipper to answer, she said, "I was thinking, maybe we should report that Chow who was throwing bottles at us to the police."

"Right," Kipper said. "We could stop by the station after work..." But when she tried to picture it, the image was too ludicrous to seriously consider. She imagined Petra describing the scene from that morning to a blue uniformed German Shepherd taking scrupulous notes. "*Now, what kind of bottle did the Chow throw at you?*" The Shepherd would ask the questions, while an Airedale leaned against a desk toying with his beard. As soon as they left, the cop-dogs would laugh their heads off at the silly cats and dump the scrupulous notes in the wastepaper basket. Nothing would get done. Unless the cops decided to try their paws at intimidating Petra out of running for representative.

No, Petra and Kipper would have to handle any hostile dogs they had to face alone. "No. No, cops," Kipper said.

Petra shrugged. "Fine by me. It's no skin off of my nose if a Chow gets a bit hot under the collar."

"Unless the bottle *hits* you in the nose," Kipper grumbled, but Petra seemed to have completely forgotten the extent of the danger they'd been in that morning. If she'd ever been aware of it at all. In fact, she seemed to be ignoring dangers of *all* sorts. She had her photocopy of Violet's scribbled notes out and was waving it around for anyone to see. "Put that away!" Kipper hissed, grabbing her sister's paws and pressing them, with the potentially incriminating document, in toward Petra's body, shielding the page from any prying eyes.

Petra flattened her ears at Kipper and spat through her whiskers, but she still folded the page back up and stuffed it in a pocket. "What's the big deal?" Petra asked. "It's just a piece of paper with some random handwriting on it."

Petra had a point. But those cryptic notes in loopy handwriting gave Kipper the creeps. "Just keep it out of sight, okay?"

Petra shrugged and headed back to her desk. Kipper headed back to her own desk as well. Petra was already ears down in work as

Kipper passed by, but she said, without looking up, "Give Alistair a call. See if he'll meet us at Hell tonight."

So, before settling back to her important work of balancing accounts, making sure expenses were properly charged, and other fun accounting details, Kipper phoned up their brother. He was more than happy to meet his sisters at *All Cats Go To Hell*, one of the rattiest bars in New LA, that evening.

"We can go over campaign strategies," he said, looking relaxed and a bit blurry on the cheap work vid-phone. Alistair was more interested in the actual politics of Petra's campaign than either of his sisters.

"Maybe," Kipper answered, looking over at her sister. "Petra's being kind of off-the-wall today." It looked like Petra was still puzzling over Violet's notes, instead of working. "She thinks she's found a set of secret instructions to a cat sanctuary down in Ecuador."

"Seems unlikely."

Alistair's simple, pragmatic response made sense, but Kipper had to admit she liked Petra's completely unrealistic obsession a little better. The idea of a cat haven in Ecuador, unlikely though it might be, made her feel like there was a backdoor to this dog eat cat world. A secret ticket out, if things got too rough.

Chapter 3

After Kipper finished her exciting day of balancing accounts, and Petra finished her last-minute canvassing of the water-cooler dogs, the two sisters headed down to their favorite hangout, deep in the heart of Old Town. The bus ride between Luna Tech and All Cats Go To Hell was short and, unlike that morning, uneventful. The walk from the bus stop to the bar's front door, however, always made Kipper a little nervous. And tonight she was extra jumpy, seeing shadows everywhere.

Behind Petra's cheerful chatter about how they should go down to Ecuador themselves and find out what Violet was up to, Kipper could hear dogs talking in the alleyways. Their laughter echoed off the dilapidated brick walls, punctuated by the cooing, purrful propositions of gaudily dressed, faux Siamese and Bengals sashaying along the streets.

They even passed a cat who had herself done up as a Siberian tiger—all black and orange and white. She was probably naturally black, because the orange and white were obviously fake. It made Kipper feel embarrassed to be a cat. But she also worried for the sakes of these poor cats. Street cats generally didn't live long lives.

As if all that weren't enough, Kipper had the distinct feeling that someone was following them. Every now and then, she saw a large, black shadow out of the corner of her eye and she heard a heavy echo to her footsteps. But it was probably nothing more than the giant, crumbling, human buildings playing with the sound and light.

Kipper was relieved when the small, cozy shape of All Cats Go To Hell nestled inside one of the ancient First Race ruins came into sight ahead of them.

The bar didn't look like much. The red neon sign had a few missing letters, and the front window had a few broken panes... But, the food was good and, unquestionably, Sammy the bartender whipped up the *best* milk froths in New LA. That's what made All Cats Go To Hell worth the trouble.

Sammy, ironically, was a dog, but none of the cats held it against him. He was a tall but beanpole thin mutt, and his golden eyes were everything a bartender's should be: soulful, inviting, and sympathetic. Even the most diffident cat would confide in Sammy, and Sammy would nod his speckled head, tutting sympathetically at the cat's problems.

Alistair had beaten his sisters there and was already relaxing on a barstool, making small talk with Sammy. When he saw them come in, Alistair ordered one straight froth for Kipper and a double froth with a shot of caramel for Petra. That had been her drink since early kittenhood; Petra had always had a sweet tooth.

"Hey Kip; Pet," Alistair greeted his sisters. "Let's take our drinks and get a table."

Kipper followed her brother docilely; Petra, however, bounced between at least three extra tables greeting cats and dogs she knew. Only after Kipper and Alistair were settled did Petra let the steaming, foaming drink waiting for her at their table draw her back to them.

"So," Petra said, taking her seat, "did the Kipster tell you? We're forgetting this whole election thing and heading to Ecuador."

"Um... yeah..." Alistair answered, "she told me something about it..."

Within minutes, Petra and Alistair were deep in a one-sided debate about the importance of her running for district representative. One-sided because Petra's wild plans involving Ecuador were hardly coherent enough to call an argument. Kipper had heard Alistair's organized, orderly, and logical arguments before, and she soon found herself zoning out of the conversation.

Her eyes kept being drawn back to a large, black dog with brown eyebrows and muzzle sitting at the far corner table. Kipper couldn't make out her breed—something between black lab and Rottweiler. If it weren't for the incident with the flying bottles and broken glass less than twelve hours before, Kipper probably wouldn't have thought twice about yet another dog big enough to pin her with one paw. As it was, she kept wondering if this was the large, black shadow that had been following her.

That Chow had really shaken her up. Kipper tried to shake it off and put the scary dog sitting in the corner out of her mind. She tried to focus on what Alistair was saying.

"They're cutting the funding for New LA catteries *again.*"

Petra looked bored, but Alistair kept going.

"This is an important issue," he said. "I think you should really focus on it in your campaigning. Most of the cats around here grew up in catteries. This is an issue that will touch them."

"Yes, it touches all of us," Petra agreed, still bored and a little sardonic.

Kipper could see Petra's point. Alistair had given them each the catteries speech about a thousand times. It did get a little tiresome. Though, he was absolutely right. Kipper stared into the snowy whiteness of her drink. Thinking about catteries took Kipper back to her kittenhood. It would do the same for most cats around here.

Kipper, Alistair, and Petra had all been cattery kittens. They'd always speculated that their mother was a tortie, since Kipper was gray and the other two orange. Of course, any number of crossings could produce a litter like that, but it was nice to have an image of her. Even a made-up one. Catteries were notorious for their poor record keeping.

Alley cats, young mothers who could barely support themselves let alone an unwanted litter, brought their kittens to the catteries for a warm home with good food. The kittens got that. But they mostly grew up alone.

Many kittens were accidentally or carelessly separated from their siblings during kittenhood. Some lost their littermates to young deaths. Kipper was very lucky to have both her brother and her sister. Though, she wished she had known her mother. Alistair looked out for her; and, she and Petra stuck together; but it wasn't the same as having parents.

Unwanted kittens were a big problem in New LA. Even so, only the most liberal, generous, and desperate dog couples would adopt a kitten.

"It's a subject you can speak about from the heart," Alistair said.

"No," Petra countered, "It's a subject *you* can speak about from the heart. The subject I can speak about from the heart is *Ecuador*." And with that proclamation, Petra excused herself to the bar where she ordered another froth for herself and Kipper.

"You know," Kipper said, watching her sister wait at the bar, "I can't help thinking, Ali, that maybe you should be the one running for government." He certainly knew more about the issues, and all the cats Kipper knew liked him.

But Alistair deferred. "No, no. *Petra's* the one with the passion," he said, also watching their sister.

Kipper refrained from pointing out that while Petra had passion, it was completely unfocused.

When the froths were ready, Petra brought them over, along with a plate of game hen for them all to share. She and Kipper hadn't had dinner yet, having come straight from the office, and Alistair was always up for a snack.

As the three cats talked on, drinking and munching juicy bird, Kipper started to feel *herself* coming unfocused. The creaminess of her froth got in Kipper's whiskers, giving her a gummy feeling, but the white warmth glowed in her stomach.

About halfway through the plate of game hen and around the time Petra brought over a third round of froths, the live music started. A droopy mouthed Beagle took the stage and, seated in a spotlighted rocking chair, sang the blues. His low, baying voice was accompanied by the jangly bleat of a cat pounded piano. The music was magic to Kipper's pointed ears. She wondered if the froths had something to do with that...

"You ordered this with a shot of rum... didn't you?" she asked Petra, but instead of answering, Petra shot her a devilish grin and headed to the bar to get another round.

"I have to head off," Alistair told Kipper. "My shift starts at midnight." He worked a forklift. It wasn't a prestigious job, but it was more stable than anything Kipper had found. "Don't let Petra get you too drunk," he said. "And see that Petra makes it home?"

"Yeah, yeah," Kipper agreed, wondering why she had to be the responsible sister when it was Petra running for office. By the time she finished knocking back her rum-laced froth—in preparation for the new one Petra was already bringing her—Kipper felt her cares beginning to lift. A few sips into the fresh drink, her lightening cares took flight and flew away. Like birds flying South to Ecuador.

"Is that where birds go for the winter?" Kipper asked Petra.

"Where?" Petra asked.

"Ecuador."

"To Ecuador!" Petra answered, but it wasn't really an answer. More of a toast. So, Kipper toasted with her, "To Ecuador!"

A few sips further into their froths, Petra named the theoretical Ecuadorian cat haven "Cat Havana." Shortly after that, the sisters decided to spend next Christmas in Ecuador. Do a little bird-watching, start a worker's revolution, and make Cat Havana a reality.

Their plans were well underway when a funny looking cat with a pinched face and buggy eyes interrupted Petra's oratory on Ecuadorian, Cat-Havanian Christmas carols.

Kipper didn't think they should invite the funny cat to Cat Havana with them. "You could recruit other cats for us, though," she told him. "If you'd like."

"You don't remember me?" the funny cat asked.

Kipper flattened her ears and focused her eyes better. The funny cat wasn't a cat; he was the Chihuahua from that morning. "I'm sorry, I didn't recognize you without your cell phone." Then, narrowing her eyes, "You've got a lot of gall coming up to us after what happened this morning."

The Chihuahua fidgeted nervously with his paws. His eyes darted back and forth between the sister cats. "I didn't know Gerald was going to act like that. Really. He's a good guy. At heart..." the Chihuahua ended feebly.

Kipper's look could have withered a catnip plant, though she would have regretted it afterwards. Petra, however, invited the Chihuahua to join them. Of course, Petra, herself, was on the way to talk to a table of their co-workers across the room. She promised to be back soon.

"I think it's great you're running for office," the Chihuahua told Kipper.

"*Her*," Kipper said, indicating her disappearing sister. "She's running for office."

"Well, I'll vote for her!"

"Promising votes is cheap," Kipper grumbled into her drink, wondering why Petra always had to be so social.

"Actually," the Chihuahua said. "I came over here to make this morning up to you. See that black dog over there? By the door?"

Kipper's blood ran chill. The dog the Chihuahua meant was her black shadow from earlier. Suddenly, all the warm milk she'd been drinking turned sour in her stomach. "Yeah, I see that dog," she said.

"Well, she's been watching you all night. I'd get out of here if I were you."

"Thanks for the tip," Kipper told the Chihuahua, though she couldn't help thinking it wasn't really very helpful. Kipper could recognize a hired thug when she saw one, without any help from some ditzy Chihuahua. If he'd really wanted to make that morning up to her, he would have offered to escort her and Petra home. Not that a Chihuahua would be much protection from the big black thing in the corner...

Thinking of Petra... Where had she got to? She wasn't sitting with the water-cooler dogs at the table of their co-workers any more. Kipper didn't see her anywhere in the bar. "Did you see where my sister went?" Kipper asked the Chihuahua.

"I wasn't watching her," he said. "Maybe she was smart and slipped out."

"Without me?" Kipper asked, skeptically.

The Chihuahua shrugged. So much for dogs believing in loyalty. Well, in fairness, the Chihuahua might believe in loyalty—just not loyalty in *cats*. Kipper knew better. Petra wouldn't leave her alone here, in danger, unless Petra was in worse danger.

Kipper tipped back her milk-mug and licked the final drops of milky froth from the cool glass. The milk was room temperature, and all the fluffiness was gone. But the burn of the rum gave her courage.

"Well, good luck to you," the Chihuahua said. Then, he headed back to his table. He'd been sitting with a couple cats and another

Chihuahua—it looked like a great gang, but it only emphasized how alone Kipper now felt in that crowded barroom. Wherever Petra was, she wasn't in sight. Kipper stood up casually. She could see the black dog watching her, pretending not to watch her. So, Kipper pretended not to be aware, all the while keeping the black dog in her sights. She didn't want her back to that big brute, even in a crowded barroom.

It made it harder to get to the bathrooms, but she managed to edge along the bar and get there. Not that it did her any good. Petra wasn't there. So, she must have left the bar entirely. Kipper really was alone, and who knew what kind of state Petra was in...

Kipper hadn't seen a second dog with the big black one, but that didn't mean there wasn't one. Or more. Waiting outside. In fact, Kipper thought, that's probably what happened to Petra. Next, it would happen to her. But she wasn't going to wait for it. She didn't relish the idea of facing her big black shadow alone, but she didn't see a better alternative. Besides, if something had happened to her sister, that dog had the answer to it.

So, Kipper walked straight toward her.

The black dog was arranging coasters on the table, trying to stand them up like a card castle. *Deceptively innocent, pretending to be preoccupied.* The coasters toppled over as Kipper approached, but the black dog continued to stare at them, brown eyebrows hooding her dark eyes.

"So, is it just you and me now?" Kipper asked, figuring that whatever friends of this thug grabbed Petra, they were probably gone by now.

"I guess so," the dog answered, looking around the bar a little confusedly. Kipper picked up on her meaning: perhaps this dog was the only thug left, but there were certainly a lot of witnesses.

"Will it do any good if I stay here all night?" Kipper asked.

The dog answered, "I've nowhere else to be."

"Will it make a difference if I leave with a crowd?"

"Have you got one coming?"

Kipper took a moment to think about it. Alistair wouldn't be off his shift at the shipyard until late in the morning, and these dogs had already nabbed Petra. Her temp job kept her moving around too much to make any real friends at work, and Petra's work friends were already gone. "Well, if we're going to do this," she said, feeling the fur rise along the nape of her neck, "let's get it over with."

"After you," the black dog said while rising. She gestured for Kipper to precede her to the door. Kipper felt wary of letting the dog follow her from behind, but she didn't think the dog would attack until they were outside. And Kipper had an idea.

She could feel the dog's warm breath on her ears as she walked through the crowd toward the barroom door. The crowd thinned before they reached the door, and Kipper felt the coolness that the last customer to walk through that door had let in.

Kipper pushed the door open, stepped out, and as she rounded the edge, she flung the wooden slab of a door back with all her strength. The door slammed hard into the black dog's wet nose, and Kipper dropped into a crouch on the other side. She could hear laughter from inside the bar. She hadn't realized anyone was watching. Maybe they'd come out to help? She didn't think so...

The black dog didn't take long to recover. She grumbled a menacing growl and launched herself out the door to the find Kipper. But Kipper was still ducked under her line of sight. The black menace was still gawking frantically about looking for her striped cat target, perfectly camouflaged in the gray night, when a blur of stripes launched itself at her knees, clawing and tripping her.

Because of her massive size, relative to Kipper, the black dog went down hard. But, Kipper still took the worst of it, since she was too entangled to get away. The black dog crumpled her like a stone falling on a paper bag. A tussle of paws and claws ensued, leading to the black dog rising from the ground, Kipper clamped firmly in her massy paws.

Bright lines of blood sprang up on the dog's muzzle as Kipper clawed her, but that only caused the dog to hurl Kipper away from her, toward one of the crumbling brick walls of the ruin around the bar. *Thud!* Kipper's body hit the wall. *Crack!* Her neck whiplashed her head against the bricks. Her furry body crumpled to the hard ground in a cloud of dust from the ancient mortar.

Dull aches and sharp pains wandered over Kipper's body as if they were surveying her like a piece of land, trying to find the best place to settle down. Eventually, the dull aches congregated to her back, and the sharp pains set up homesteads between the roots of her ears and in her right arm.

Kipper forced herself up from the ground, and the dog was waiting for her. Kipper unsheathed her claws and raised her left arm to swipe, but the world grew dark and dizzy. She lost her footing and, shakily, ended up back on the ground. Her body had taken almost as much as it could take, and it was time to try reasoning with the dog now. If Kipper could only force her whirling mind around it...

"She won't stand down," Kipper said and immediately regretted it. She'd meant to lie, but her brain had forgotten that between forming the thought and transmitting the words to her tongue. "I mean, *she will* stand down." She put her paw to her head, ashamed at how hollow the lie sounded. With a little more conviction she said, "I'll convince my sister to back out of the election."

"Election?" the dog asked.

"Yeah..." Kipper answered, and, in her wobbly state, she launched into one of Petra's rehearsed campaign speeches, babbling about funding and initiatives, before realizing the problem. "You don't know about the election?"

The black dog looked deeply puzzled, and her brown eyebrows were pinched into an expression of concern.

"What do you want, if you don't know about the election?" Kipper couldn't tell if it was the rum or the pain that was making her brain foggy. She decided to believe it was the pain and was thankful for her foresight in drinking so much natural painkiller.

For a moment, Kipper even wondered if she had picked a fight with this brute of a dog for no reason. Could she be that drunk? Maybe Petra wasn't always the rash, irrational one...

"I was hired to kill you," the dog said, and the words opened Kipper's mind. She knew it would make dogs mad—Petra running for office—but, it shouldn't make them *that* mad. They all lived in a much worse world than she'd thought. The dog added, "I didn't ask why."

"Funny," Kipper said, still in a daze. "That's the first thing I would have asked if someone asked me to kill someone."

The dog looked abashed. "The reasons never seemed that

important when I was, you know, just roughing the cats up."

Kipper eyed her skeptically, as if to ask, "*Is that a hobby you indulge in often?*"

"You know..." the dog said. Then, making her voice gruff, presumably in imitation of her employer, "Send such and such tomcat a message: keep out of my part of the town." Back in her normal voice, she ended, "It's all kind of silly, really."

And that was precisely the attitude that let this kind violence happen. "Not to the cats that you're *roughing up*," Kipper said.

The dog's face contorted, her ears far back and her muzzle parted in a nervous look of distress. "I can see that now."

The big black dog looked Kipper over, clearly unused to seeing the bloodied results of her work. Her eyes could not have looked more guilty. Kipper shifted and shivered, the cold earth numbing her limbs. The dog crouched down beside her and felt her for broken bones.

"You'll be okay," the dog said, transitioning from would-be assassin to nursemaid. The change made Kipper's mind reel, but, when the dog offered her a paw to help her up, Kipper took it. She swooned as she rose, but the dog's strong black paws held her firm and walked her to a car parked down the street.

In the car, the dog, whose name was Trudith, fed Kipper an aspirin, apologized, felt Kipper's forehead for a fever, apologized, dusted off Kipper's fur, and apologized again. Under Trudith's sisterly affection and solicitation, Kipper broke down and cried. "Why do they want to kill me? Petra's only trying to make things better! And why don't any of the other cats see that? None of them even seem to care... Not even Petra..." Kipper's cat dignity took over again, but she could see the pitiful cat act was working on Trudith. She sniffled and let out her pain in a piteous mew.

"It makes me so mad!" Trudith said. Her brown eyebrows were arched in anger, and the two animals shared a pregnant silence. While Trudith stewed over all the injustices Kipper had so vividly painted for her, Kipper wracked her brain to understand her sudden change in fortune. It *couldn't* be about the election, and, although Petra had a way of making people angry at her, she didn't have any real enemies. Just enmity from passing strangers. Certainly nothing bad enough to set anyone out to kill her or her sister...

"Give me a minute..." Trudith said, storming out of the car. Kipper could see her black, lumbering shape walk back to the bar and climb into the phone booth beside it. In her moment of solitude, Kipper patted herself down, feeling the rough, comfort of the clothes covering her body. Her paw happened on the lump in her vest pocket. She pulled out the rumpled, scribbly sheet she'd found at work, on Violet's desk. Was this was the key? To everything that was happening? Or was it just the muzziness of the rum that made Ecuador and Petra's imaginary cat haven there seem so important?

Kipper had to think... It was hard, but she worked her way back through the day. The only people who knew about Violet's ticket receipt were her, Alistair, Petra, and... *Sahalie*.

When Trudith returned, Kipper asked her, "Do you work for a dog? *Or a cat?*"

"A cat lady," Trudith said.

"Is she tabby?"

"Never saw her, never will." Suddenly, Trudith looked very proud, "I *quit*. Told that cold-hearted cat lady that she could get another dog to do her dirty work."

Trudith must have seen the look of devastation on Kipper's face, but she misinterpreted it as having to do with her failing to answer the question. "She has a nice purrful voice," Trudith said. "Could have been a tabby. Would you like her number?"

"You quit *now?*"

Trudith nodded.

"In the payphone?!"

"Yeah..." Worry had returned to Trudith's eyes. "Did I do something wrong again?"

Kipper hissed the answer between clenched teeth: "If they know I'm not dead, they're going to send someone else to kill me." Not *they*, Kipper realized. *Sahalie.*

Suddenly Kipper's brain was clearing up fast. Whatever took Violet to Ecuador had to be more than a family emergency—and Kipper would have bet her whiskers that Sahalie knew something about it. That whole scene in her office had played wrong, and Kipper couldn't put her paws on why. But now she was beginning to get a good idea: who better to embezzle funds from a company than its head accountant? But where were the funds going? And what was so important that it was worth killing to cover it up?

More importantly, where was Petra? And was she swept up in this too?

Kipper looked over at Trudith, leaning over the steering wheel with big sad eyes. "I'm so sorry," Trudith was saying. "I'm not a bad dog. It's just... The cat lady sounded so nice, and she paid me so well... It's hard to believe a thing could be wrong when someone's telling you to do it so firmly. Can I ever make this up to you?"

Sometimes Kipper couldn't believe how easy dogs were to manipulate. She'd always considered herself above manipulating dogs before, but right now she desperately needed an ally. And, luckily, this dog was already on her side.

Kipper turned to Trudith and said, "I need you to help me find my sister." She said it firmly.

A cat would have asked questions; Trudith eagerly agreed.

Kipper wondered if it seemed strange to Trudith to now be taking orders from her former target. If it did, Trudith didn't show it. Kipper supposed that as a professional thug, Trudith was simply used to taking sudden, unexplained orders—and now Kipper was the cat giving those orders. It was a job that would never suit a cat, even if the cat were big enough and strong enough to do it.

Chapter 4

After a quick sweep of the alleys surrounding the bar, Kipper thankfully concluded that Petra wasn't lying bleeding to death in any of them. Though, even with a big black dog tailing her, watching her back, Kipper still felt like jumping at every shadow. And her heart stopped when she saw a crumpled bag beside some trash bins—in the dark, it could have been her sister. But Trudith was very reassuring and convinced Kipper that if anything had happened to Petra—if thugs had dragged her out of the bar or caught up with her outside—she would still be pretty close. Close enough that they would have found her.

The obvious next step was to check Petra's apartment. Kipper didn't think she would have gone home without telling her, but she had been pretty drunk. Besides, it was the best scenario Kipper could think of, so she held onto that hope and directed Trudith on how to drive there.

Petra's apartment was on the fifth floor, and the elevator ride felt like it took forever. The hallway was eerily silent. When Kipper tried the door, it was unlocked. But, that didn't necessarily mean anything... Petra could be careless sometimes... She opened the door and stepped in.

The room was a wreck. Clothes, belongings strewn everywhere. Kipper froze. Horrible images flashed before her, and there was no telling how long she would have stood there, panic-stricken and stupefied, if Trudith hadn't come along.

"This doesn't look like a professional job," Trudith said. She was going through the things on the floor. She kept glancing at Kipper, clearly gauging her reaction. "If I didn't know any better," Trudith said, "I'd think your sister was just a very messy cat."

"Well... she is," Kipper admitted. "But..."

"Hey, I found something," Trudith said, displaying a slightly crumpled (Trudith had stepped on it with her big paws) piece of paper. It had scrawled on it, in Petra's paw: *GONE TO ECUADOR! BACK SOON.*

Kipper reached for it: this note was a connection—cryptic and tenuous though it might be—with her missing sister. "That's for me. It's got to be."

Maps ran through Kipper's head: she envisioned the Pacific coast of California, flowing down to Mexico, trailing, finally, into South America. And, yes, right there, at the top of the continent was where Petra had gone. Where she needed to go to find her. Roads could take her there; she didn't need planes that would leave a trail, like the trail Violet had left. The trail Petra was following. "I wonder how Petra is getting there..." Kipper said to herself. She hoped Petra was safe. Then, turning to Trudith, "I'm going to Ecuador. I have to find her."

Trudith shifted her paws; an excited whine threatened to leak from her mouth. "How will you find her?"

"I don't know. I guess I'll meet her in Ecuador," Kipper said. "That's what the note implies, right? And it's not like I know how to find her anywhere along the way..." Though Kipper realized that she was harboring a secret hope that as soon as she set off, she'd find herself traveling right behind Petra. And, then, right alongside her. "Will you drive me?"

Trudith looked at Kipper like she'd asked her how to build a rocket ship while doing brain surgery. *Completely overwhelmed.*

"I mean," Kipper said, "*Drive me.* Okay?"

"Right..." Trudith started to recompose herself. "Okay." With another moment for it to sink in, Trudith started to get excited. "We're going to Ecuador!" In bizarre contrast to her confusion of only moments before, Trudith suddenly became extremely competent and practical.

If the two road-trippers had any hope of catching Petra, they'd have to move fast. Furthermore, Trudith pointed out that whoever messed up Petra's apartment could be over at Kipper's right now. So, as much as Kipper wanted to stop by and pick up a change of her own clothes before skipping town, she had to agree it was too dangerous. In fact, they were already back in Trudith's car and blocks down the street before she pulled herself together enough to think of grabbing some clothes of Petra's. They'd already lost their edge, but maybe they could regain it by moving fast. Kipper felt like she'd be holding her breath until they made it across the Mexican border.

Trudith put the car in gear; they turned onto the freeway; and cruised out of New LA.

The ten lanes of concrete were dead in the dark of night, and Trudith's headlights were the only light around. It was rumored that the freeways in the area had remained unchanged since the time of humans, except for normal maintenance and repainting the white, yellow, and dotted lines. It was also rumored that the freeway was only six lanes wide, total, back then.

Corroded, rust orange skeletons of human cars had been found in junkyards and among the ruined human cities. The dinosaur cars were monsters compared to today's vehicles. Just like human buildings. Just like humans themselves. Kipper couldn't understand why dogs worshipped them, waiting for them to return. If humans had been so great, they wouldn't have left cats—that is, *the world*—in the condition it was in. They wouldn't have taken off into space and just *abandoned* everyone. Kipper could feel the darkness making her thoughts morbid.

Kipper drowsed off, finally, fatigued from the fight and from fighting the pain. She was greeted in her sleep by strange visions of the hairless race that came before them and threaded the world with concrete. Gibbering monkeys handed her toy rockets and pressed around her, scaring her, telling her she had to get into space—though, Kipper didn't know how she understood their gibbering language—until she frightened herself awake.

"We're ten miles from the border," Trudith said. She exuded a calm, steadiness with her driving. Kipper decided that she liked having a chauffer.

"Is there a town?" Kipper asked, rubbing the sleepers from her eyes, and gingerly stretching the stiffness from her limbs. She immediately regretted the latter when it fired up all the pain from her bruises again.

"Actually, we're driving through Saniego now," Trudith said. "Would you like to stop?"

Kipper looked out the car window, but the early morning darkness and the sound-absorbent concrete walls lining the freeway kept her from seeing any city. She would have to take Trudith's word for it. "We need maps," Kipper said. "I don't know how long it'll take us to drive all the way through Mexico."

To Kipper's utter surprise, Trudith already knew the answer. Score two for this dog's competence. "It'll take four or five days of solid driving to get to Ecuador," Trudith answered. "You can drive, right?"

"I didn't realize Mexico was so long..." Kipper said, wondering how Petra was traveling. At the same time, she was eyeing Trudith sidewise, trying to figure out if she could really expect this *dog* to stick by her the whole way. "We'll need supplies," Kipper said. "Though, we might be better off stopping for them on the other side of the border."

Trudith was quiet for a while, and Kipper began to fear that this was where she would bow out. You can't rely on dogs. But, when Trudith spoke, all she said was, "Let's stop here. I need to charge up the car." Trudith began changing lanes as soon as she saw an exit sign that advertised enough fast food places and car-charge stations to imply a hub of non-suburbia civilization.

"What confuses me," Kipper said, trying to rekindle a neutral, friendly conversation, "is why you know, off the top of your head, how far it is to Ecuador."

"Easy," Trudith replied, slowing the car down as they eased back onto city streets. "I drove there a couple years ago for the winter holidays. It was a great road trip."

"Really? But, why Ecuador? What's so special there?"

Trudith let her eyes stray from the road to give Kipper a searching look. "You really don't know? The Space Elevator is off the coast of Ecuador, between Ecuador and the Galapagos Islands."

"Holy catnip... Violet *did* go into space." Kipper had thought that was one of Petra's wilder theories.

Kipper pulled the scribbled note out of her tunic pocket. Sure enough, the first instruction was "@ SE, ask for Chip." *SE meant Space Elevator!* And if Violet went into space... And Petra was following Violet... And Kipper was following Petra... Maybe, just maybe, this paranoid nightmare would end up turning into a dream come true. She'd meet up with Petra in Ecuador, and the two of them would swash a buckle right through otter land.

"Who's Violet?" Trudith asked, maneuvering the car into a charging berth.

Kipper explained to Trudith about Violet and the scribbled notes. "If Petra is following Violet's directions, she'll head straight for the space elevator. So, that's where I'll find her." Simply saying those words made Kipper feel tingly all over.

"I need to call my brother," Kipper realized, "and tell him what's happened."

So, while Trudith parked the car in the charging berth, Kipper found a payphone on the street corner. She punched in Alistair's number on the sticky keypad. Three rings, maybe four, and Alistair's machine would pick up. Kipper was preparing herself to leave a message, but halfway through the first ring, Alistair picked up.

"Kipper?" he said. His grainy image on the payphone screen looked worried and harried.

"You're back from your night shift early," Kipper said.

"I got a weird call from Petra," he said. "I figured she was drunk somewhere, so I went looking for you. Thought we'd find her and straighten her out together. But you weren't home, and when I got to Petra's, her place was a wreck. But no sign of her."

"I'm so sorry," Kipper said. "I should have left a note for you."

"You were there?"

"I went looking for her too. There was this incident with this big black dog..." Kipper glanced over her shoulder and saw Trudith still charging the car. "But we don't need to get into that now. There was a note for me at Petra's. She's going to Ecuador."

"Ecuador?"

"Yes, Ali. She's following the tracks of that cat I was temping for—Violet."

"Why in dognation would she want to do that?"

Alistair looked really worried and frustrated. His first impulse was to fly down and meet them in Ecuador. Short of that, he wanted to involve the police. Kipper wasn't so sure that was a good idea. But, clearly, Alistair needed something to do. He had to feel like he was helping out his sisters. So, she convinced him that the best thing he could do was to take over Petra's campaign. He was a better fit for district representative anyway. Oh, and wire them some money.

Kipper promised to call him again when she could.

Trying not to dwell on her conversation with Alistair, Kipper started thinking about the next leg of their trip. The car was almost done charging, and Trudith was rummaging around in the trunk. Kipper walked up around her and leaned against the bumper, under the looming door to the trunk. "Do you think they'll be looking for me at the border?" she asked.

Trudith stopped rummaging. She looked worried. "I hadn't thought of that," she said. "Maybe we should hide you in the trunk?"

"They might check the trunk," Kipper said, but her real concern was that Trudith would forget her there. Or she would get buried under all of Trudith's luggage. "Do you keep all your stuff in here?"

"You never know when a job will take you out of town. So, I'm always prepared." Trudith looked Kipper up and down. "I don't think my clothes will fit you though. So, we'll have to buy you some changes of your own."

Kipper tried to imagine herself wearing clothes built big enough for Trudith. At best, she would look like a clown. At worst, the clothes would drag and snag and trip her up. *And* she'd look like a clown. A cat clown. The latter was more likely. "But, seriously," Kipper said, "I'm not hiding in the trunk."

Trudith found the suitcase she'd been looking for and, after waiting for Kipper to stand back, swung the trunk shut. "Then you'll have to dye your fur."

Kipper coughed as if the idea of dyed fur literally caught in her throat, like a psychological hairball. What was it today with dogs suggesting that she dye her fur?

"Seriously," Trudith said, "if they're looking for you, they're looking for a tabby cat. They won't check your ID, since you're with me." It was true that cats didn't have to show ID when an accompanying dog vouched for them—an outdated, demeaning, but, in this case, doggarned convenient law. "*Unless* you look like a cat they're looking for. So, bleach your fur white and put in some blue contacts. The border guards will barely look at you if you do that. Deaf cats make us nervous."

"That's strange. Why?"

"You can yell at 'em all you want, and it won't do any good. How are you supposed to handle them?"

Kipper flinched at Trudith's reasoning but decided to let it pass. Similarly, despite strong aesthetic reservations, Kipper agreed to bleach her fur. They got back in Trudith's car and began the search for an all-night drugstore or a similar kind of establishment. Anywhere that sold contacts and dye. Ideally, it would be nice to find a place that sold food for the road and a change of clothes to replace Kipper's dirtied and torn up vest and pants too. Still, they would take what they could get, since it was barely even morning. Dawn had not yet cracked the sky.

The two adventurers lucked out. There was a 24-hour McFriskers open. McFriskers would have everything the two of them needed. Kipper wanted to be involved in picking out the snacks and her change of clothes, but the instructions on the box of Persian Silver she picked up claimed that she had to leave the dye in her fur for a full hour. She didn't think she'd leave it in that long, but, either way, she'd better get started.

"Pick out something with long sleeves, if you can," Kipper said. "I don't know how well I'll be able to dye my arms and legs." Kipper and Trudith parted ways at the cash register, and Kipper disappeared into the McFriskers bathroom with her box of fur dye.

Ten minutes later, Kipper had the gooey gel worked into the fur on her face, head, neck, and paws. She even rolled up her pants legs and lathered the goo up to her knees; on her arms, she had it past her elbows. She looked a fright, but she tried not to think about it. She tried not to think about how long it would take for her fur to shed and regrow...

The Persian Silver box said the chemicals in the dye worked

better with heat, so she kept the wall-mounted blow-dryer running. Every time it stopped, she pushed in the big silver button again. It was only meant for drying paws, so Kipper had to keep contorting herself to get the blast of heat all over her body. She kept worrying that another cat—or a dog, but that would be less petrifying— would come in and see her awkward acrobatics. It was a miserable half hour. The results weren't much better.

When Kipper couldn't take it anymore, she did her best to rinse the dye out in the sink. Getting the back of her head and her lower paws under the stream of water from the faucet turned out to be much more challenging than heating those parts of her body with the blow-dryer. When she gave up, her fur still felt greasy with the gel.

Kipper was staring at herself, numbly, in the bathroom mirror when Trudith came in, holding a bundle of clothes.

"I put the food and some more clothes in the car," she said. "But, I thought you might like to change in here."

"Thanks," Kipper said. She couldn't believe what she'd just done to herself. She looked like a ghost. Or the victim of an industrial accident. "I don't think this is going to work."

Trudith looked puzzled. "Why not? You're white. When you put the contacts in, no one will know the difference if you're stripey under your clothes. Here," Trudith shoved the clothes toward her, "put these on."

Kipper continued to be amazed by the obtuseness of dogs. Her fur looked ashen and streaky. The corners of her old gray showed through like scorch marks.

But the guards at the border would be dogs. If Trudith couldn't tell the difference between her and a real white cat, then she guessed they had a chance. Kipper sighed at her washed out image in the mirror—*nothing* like *Persian Silver*, more like dirty, day old, tread upon snow—and took the bundle of clothes into one of the bathroom stalls to change.

Miraculously, Trudith had chosen clothes that fit. They were too loose, but that was better than too tight. And the pants had a drawstring, so they did stay on. At least, once Kipper cinched the drawstring as tight as it would go. Had they been designed for a

Pug, perhaps? Or some other kind of solid, stout, barrel-chested dog with short legs? Well, they would do. It was just lucky Kipper had got her arms and legs dyed as much as she had. Trudith may have picked her out a long-sleeved tunic, but the arms still only made it halfway past her elbows.

Trudith did seem to have a decent sense of color, and that was something. The trousers were muted shades of somber brown, and the tunic was a blue to match her eyes. Well, it was a blue to match her contacts anyway. They were not colors she would look good in usually, but it was the perfect completion of her blue-eyed, white-cat costume.

Back in the car, on the freeway, the sun was tipping the horizon in gold. Trudith drummed her paws on the steering wheel and kept glancing over at Kipper. "I just can't get over it," she said, her voice louder than usual. "It's hard to believe you're not really, you know, deaf."

Kipper rolled her eyes and flattened her ears. Maybe if she ignored Trudith for long enough, Trudith *would* start believing it. And stop talking to her.

"Just pretend you can't hear me, okay?"

Kipper wondered whether it would help with the illusion if Trudith didn't act like she expected Kipper to hear her. However, she decided that Trudith would probably talk to a real deaf cat anyway. No worries. If Kipper played her part, the dogs wouldn't be thrown by Trudith. So, Kipper stared out the window and held her ears straight forward, as if there wasn't a sound in the world for them to turn and detect. Trudith prattled on.

Otters in Space

Chapter 5

The guard flicked his ears in the chill desert air. Mornings were cold, but it would be hot when the sun got overhead and started beating down. During the day, it was no place for the thick, full mane of a rough Collie; but, right now, it was a bit nippy for a smooth one. The guard dog scratched the barrel of his rifle against his chin. A car was coming.

The gleaming black sedan slowed as it approached. The guard dog could see a black dog driving inside, dressed in a sharp, black vest, sunglasses, and a red bandana tied at her throat. An angry looking, white cat was sitting at the dog's side. It was a shame, having a white cat like that in such a fancy, black car. The cat would get white hair all over the lovingly burnished upholstery.

The car came to stop, and the window rolled down. "Can I see some ID?" the guard said.

Trudith handed over her wallet, flipped open to her license.

"Where're you going?" the guard asked, looking past Trudith at the white cat. The white cat stared resolutely out the window. "Who's your friend?"

Trudith looked over at Kipper, like she expected Kipper to answer. But Kipper didn't even move her eyes. She'd picked a sign on the guard booth beside the road and was reading it over and over again. "*All Unaccompanied Cats Must Carry Proof Of Employment.*" Were unemployed cats such a huge problem in Mexico?

"We're just heading down to Tiawaana," Trudith said. "The cat's my assistant. Her name's, uh, Sylvia." Trudith cuffed Kipper on the shoulder, so Kipper turned toward her. Her blue eyes were an icy glare, and she rapidly moved her paws through a pantomime of deaf-cat signing she once saw. It wouldn't fool a deaf cat, but it might fool a normal one. So, it should certainly fool a dog.

"What's she saying?" the guard asked.

"I, uh..." Trudith stared at Kipper's paws intently. "I think she was just asking what's taking so long." Trudith looked back at the guard, who was now examining her license. "I only hired Sylvia a few weeks ago. I'm still getting the hang of her signing."

"Sure," the guard said. "What do you need a deaf cat for to assist you?"

"She does the books," Trudith said, far too flippantly for Kipper's taste.

The guard dog narrowed his eyes and shifted his glance between Trudith and Kipper. "Hey, Sylvia," the guard dog shouted. "You got any ID?"

Kipper strained every fiber of her self-control to keep from flattening her ears. Her nose wrinkled a little in spite of herself, but she didn't think the guard dog could see.

"Whaddayou want ID for?" Trudith asked. "She's my cat. Are you insulting me?"

The guard dog grumbled, a low growl. "I'll be back," he said. "I just have to check on something." With that, he walked around the sedan and disappeared into the guard booth, shaking his head over Trudith's ID.

In the car, Trudith's ears were flat back. Their rounded ends always flopped by the side of her head, but the muscles at their base were strained. Her jowly, brown muzzle was tight shut, making her look stricken. "He can't have recognized you," she said to herself. "I can hardly recognize you." Trudith looked over at Kipper, reassuring herself that Kipper was absolutely unmistakable for a gray tabby cat. "Maybe there's a white cat wanted for murder down here..." Trudith pondered the ridiculous possibility. "If I have to," she said. "I'll fight to protect you. I can take a Collie. He's just a herd-dog, even if he is a big one."

Behind her random babbling, Trudith looked as nervous as a

kitten, but Kipper dared not either console or mock her. The guard dog could emerge at any moment, and she couldn't risk being overheard. Trudith reached over, grabbed, and squeezed Kipper's paw, as if Kipper was the one who was afraid. She withdrew her paw quickly when the Collie returned.

"Your license expired a month ago," the guard Collie said.

Trudith's eyes widened in terror. Her cat was about to be caught and turned over to the evil tabby who was chasing her, and it would be Trudith's fault for not getting her license renewed. "That's not Sylvia's fault!" she blurted out.

The guard dog gave her the strangest look, but he decided to dismiss her outburst. Black lab mutts weren't always the brightest. "It's just a formality to renew it," he said. "Would you like me to punch the renewal into my computer?"

Trudith looked flustered, but then her jowls broke into a relieved grin. "Yah," she said. "Do that. And I'll make sure Sylvia does a better job keeping me up to date on my paperwork. Right Sylvia?"

Again, Trudith seemed to have forgotten that, according to her role as *Sylvia*, Kipper couldn't hear. But, no harm was done. Ignoring Trudith came naturally to Kipper by now.

After they pulled away from the guard station, safely inside Mexico, Kipper took her contacts out. She was pleased to discover that Trudith's tone of voice returned to normal with the change in her eye color.

About an hour down the road, Kipper realized that Trudith's banter was losing the slim grip on coherency that it originally had. "Then the otter jumped in the river and swam away! Right there in the space station. Those are some crazy space stations the otters have."

"Trudith, would you like me to drive?" Kipper asked. "I slept most of the way to Saniego, but you've been awake all night."

Trudith drove on, quietly thinking the question through. Kipper was getting used to the fact that Trudith took longer to think about things than she expected. It contrasted strangely with her ability to bellow on and on, telling stories about the places she'd been and the fights she'd started. "Yeah," Trudith eventually said. "Do you mind if we stop, and I lie down in the back?" When Trudith looked over,

Kipper could see that her eyes were red-rimmed and bleary. Kipper would feel safer without her behind the wheel.

After a quick roadside lesson in handling Trudith's vehicle, Kipper adjusted the seat to accommodate her smaller stature. She had to slide the chair almost all the way forward for her feet to reach the pedals. Nonetheless, it was a nice car. A *very* nice car.

When Kipper had learned to drive, she'd had to borrow Alistair's car. It was an old junker he'd bought from a dog who was going to literally take it to the junkyard. Alistair had fixed the car up, and he used it to get around. He insisted on teaching both Petra and Kipper to drive, even though they both took the bus. He said they never knew when it would come in useful. Kipper guessed he was right.

Once she could hear Trudith's snuffly snoring emanating from the back seat, Kipper felt herself liberated. She was driving the nicest car she'd ever driven, cruising down mile after mile of an empty stretch of freeway. The speedometer went twice as high as Trudith had pushed it, and Kipper wanted to drive this car for all it was worth. So, she eased her foot into the accelerator and felt real speed. At this rate, she could halve the time to Ecuador.

Kipper pretended the black sedan was her own spaceship, bought at a criminally low rate from an aging otter. The aging otter had only used it for Sunday commutes to visit his grandpups on Kelp Frond station, so it was in perfect, stellar, starhopping condition. For the first couple hours, Kipper bounced her razor-cool spaceship off the gravity well of Mars and dodged it, at record speeds, through the asteroid belt. Otters were fast, but a cat can be even faster. Dogs are for Earth; otters for the oceans. Truly, it's cats who are meant for space.

Of course, racing spaceships against otters (and beating the otters mercilessly, she might add) probably wasn't what Petra had in mind when she took off for Ecuador. If Petra thought this goose chase was worth abandoning her campaign for, she probably thought there was a greater cause at stake. Perhaps a place for every cat in space, not just her and Kipper.

There was a thought. Forget Cat Havana in Ecuador... Kipper would rather hold out for a Cat Havana on a space station. Is that where Violet was going? Kipper was pretty sure that Violet was headed for space, but could Petra still be right too? Kipper could picture it—Violet, up among the stars and the otters, on a space station for cats, and cats alone.

No, a cat space station was too much of a long shot. It would have been in the otters' newscasts, and Kipper would have heard about it. She religiously watched otter news. Violet's motive had to be something else. And, based on Kipper's recent experiences, *something dangerous*. Not something wonderful.

A terrible thought struck her, and Kipper had to work to keep her eyes on the road and paws on the wheel. Could Violet be dead? Was Violet dead? She'd bought a plane ticket... That didn't mean she'd made it to the plane. Not necessarily.

Oh my. What *had* Violet done to upset Sahalie? Whatever it was, Sahalie thought it was worth killing two cats to cover it up. Double caticide; attempted, anyway. Sahalie had to have backed herself into a corner and backed herself in bad.

Scared as she was, Kipper honestly felt sorry for Sahalie that she'd gotten herself into a situation so bad that she thought hiring an assassin to take out a fellow cat was her only way out. If dogs treated cats better, this kind of thing wouldn't happen. Cats didn't turn on each other for no reason. Dogs made them do it.

The sky was already darkening when Kipper heard Trudith rousing in the back seat. Kipper had been thinking all day, and her thoughts had begun chasing each other in circles, like puppies chasing their tails. She had worn herself out with thinking and driving, and she was ready for a break.

The two travelers stopped on the dusty stretch of road in the twilight to switch drivers and catch a bite to eat. Back in Saniego, Trudith had bought jerky steaks which they ate in silence, leaning against the side of the car, kicking their back paws in the dirt. It was good to stretch their legs. Though, every car that passed made Kipper's heart leap. She strained her eyes looking for Petra, but she only saw dogs behind the wheels.

Jerky steaks kept well—actually, a properly sealed jerky steak would probably outlive a tortoise on life-extending, telomerase therapy—but they were hard on Kipper's stomach. She preferred fowl and fish, but she'd been busy dying her fur when the food was selected. She would have happily traded jobs with Trudith, but dying Trudith's face and arms wouldn't have helped them at the border. On second thought, if Trudith's fur had turned out the way Kipper was imagining it, the guard might have been too shocked to do more than stare slack-jawed as they drove on.

As soon as they were back in the car, Kipper curled herself around her stomachache and fell right asleep. She dreamed about being with her sister again.

When Kipper woke up, it was day. The glare of the light hurt her eyes, but she could see that the countryside had grown lush and green while she slept. They'd left the dusty California landscape far behind. Kipper crawled into the front seat with Trudith. "Where are we?" she asked. "Is this still Mexico?"

"We're coming up on Mexico City. We may get to Guatemala by later today." As they progressed, the roads were getting worse, but Trudith made up for it by driving fast.

Kipper watched the city zoom by outside her window. It was much more crowded than New LA. More of the ancient human buildings were still standing. They stretched toward the sky like the sun bleached rib bones of an abandoned carcass. The dogs and cats had squeezed smaller, more temporary buildings around them. "Do they live in the human buildings?" Kipper asked.

"I think they build inside them," Trudith said. "They put up partitions made from old sheets and bedspreads. I went to a swap meet in one. It was hot and crowded."

"Humans left a lot more of us in Mexico than the US, didn't they?"

"More dogs than cats," Trudith said. She didn't have to connect the dots: there were fewer cats in Mexico because there were so many dogs. In a country where dogs were fighting the effects of overpopulation, cats were even worse off. It was a sobering sight. New LA looked like a ghost town in comparison. Of course, sometimes New LA felt like a ghost town anyway.

The histories weren't very good that far back, but all the evidence suggested that animals had a hard time rebuilding society after humans left. Humans had, according to their own unearthed records, controlled canine and feline breeding processes for a long time. They'd genetically engineered cats and dogs over hundreds of years, through selective breeding programs, to be the companion animals they became.

Even during the process of upraising cats and dogs to sentience, many individuals, especially in the cities, were kept incapable of reproduction to keep the society under control. The first generations of independence—after the human exodus—relied heavily on migration from the countryside and other rural areas to repopulate the cities. Only after the population stabilized could they begin maintaining the cities and rebuilding for themselves.

Kipper waited until they were past the heart of Mexico City to suggest they stop. They found a small town on the outer fringes of Mexico City where Trudith could recharge the car and Kipper could, reluctantly, call Alistair again.

"Hello?" Alistair answered his vid-phone.

He didn't recognize her, and Kipper realized it was her *white* fur. "It's me. *Kipper,*" she said.

"Oh, hi, Kip!" He tactfully didn't comment on the dyed fur. "Have you caught up with Petra?"

"Uh... Not yet," Kipper answered, surprised by how cheerful Alistair looked. "Have you heard from her?"

"Nope," he said. "But I wired the money for you. It's at the Coastal Canine Bank, in Guayaquil, Ecuador, under our mother's name. That way either of you can pick it up. In case Petra gets there first. And thinks to call home."

Kipper smiled, "Cute."

"Thanks," Alistair said.

Of course, they didn't really know their mother's name, but when they were kittens Kipper, Alistair, and Petra liked to pretend her name was Mother Theresa B. Goodkitty. No one else knew that, and there was no way to trace it to any of them.

Kipper wished Petra had checked in with Alistair. She must have had a chance by now. She could be so inconsiderate sometimes. Unless, of course, something had happened to her... Kipper quickly derailed that line of thinking. Petra was a tough cat. If any cat could take care of herself, it was Petra.

"How's the campaign going?" Kipper asked.

Alistair leaned back, looking very relaxed and pleased with himself. At least *he* didn't seem to be worried about their wayward sister. If he wasn't, maybe she shouldn't be. *Stupid Petra.*

"Excellent," Alistair said, answering her question. "The cats around here are eating it up that I took over the campaign of my poor, lost sister who's vanished without a trace. The police are freaking out, because they're taking all the heat, and they can't prove that they're not the ones who disappeared her. And you."

"Just as long as Sahalie doesn't turn on you."

"Sahalie? Isn't that Petra's boss?" Alistair looked confused. Kipper had forgotten that she hadn't had time to tell him about Sahalie during their last call.

"Yeah..." Kipper said. "She's the one who hired Trudith." *Wait... had she told him about Trudith?* Kipper couldn't remember. "But, it's okay, now she's driving me to Ecuador."

"Sahalie?" Now Alistair looked really confused.

"No, Trudith." Kipper didn't feel up to sorting the story out for him. "But..." she said, thinking it out for herself. "Sahalie shouldn't have any reason to turn on you, if you're claiming that you don't know what happened to me and Petra."

Alistair looked at Kipper like she was crazy. Kipper recognized the look. It was one they both gave Petra a lot. "Don't worry," he said. "That's my whole line: I have *no idea* what happened to you or Petra. Besides," he looked smug, "it's too late for anyone to come after me. If anything happened to me now, there'd probably be a revolution."

Kipper flicked her ears. "I told you that you were better suited to politics than Petra. Or me."

"You just keep yourself safe and catch up with Petra," he said.

Kipper hung up the vid-phone and sighed. She wished she felt as sure of everything as her brother. And she wished she'd be there to vote for him, but, at this rate, she really would make it to Ecuador before finding Petra. Kipper knew it was crazy, but she kept hoping to run into Petra at a road stop or drive past a car and suddenly recognize her driving it. Though, even if she did find Petra along the way, Kipper knew she wouldn't feel safe in New LA again until she found out what happened between Violet and Sahalie. And whether Sahalie was done trying to happen it to her. Kipper was in this one for the long haul.

Kipper walked the block back to the car charge station, but Trudith's black sedan was parked in front of the convenience store, no longer in the charger. Trudith was nowhere to be seen.

Kipper tried the car doors, but Trudith had locked them. There was a dog behind the register in the convenience store, and Kipper could see several mangy, yellow, short-haired dogs kicking a can down the street. She thought about waiting by the car, but the street dogs made her nervous. There were so few cats here, she didn't know how the dogs would treat a cat. Was she an oddity to ignore? A toy to play with? Kipper didn't want to find out, so she took a chance on the speckled dog behind the register.

The glass door chimed as she opened it, but Kipper didn't go all the way in. She stood inside the open door and shouted out, "Have you seen the black dog with the sedan?" She gestured toward Trudith's car.

The dog answered in a heavy accent that Kipper couldn't understand, but then he came out from behind the register. He put his paws on her and began forcing her back outside. Kipper felt the fur on the back of her neck rising and her claws flexing inside their sheaths. She backed away from the dog, throwing his arm off of her, but he kept walking around the edge of the store front, gesturing for her to follow. He wanted her to follow him down the alley between the stores, but Kipper didn't like the idea of being alone back there with him. She added distance between them, edging toward the other building until she could get a view down the alley, around the back of the convenience store.

It was an open field back there, and she could see about twenty dogs. Trudith was among them, fighting them off. She was clearly the biggest and the strongest—the others all looked gauntly thin in comparison—but she was no match for twenty dogs.

Kipper's teeth parted in a hiss, and she slashed at the speckled dog as he grabbed her wrist and tried to drag her toward the other dogs. She fought and spat, but the speckled dog kept talking in his incomprehensible Mexican accent and pulling her down the alley. She simply wasn't as strong as him. Even the smallest dogs are stronger than most strong cats. At the end of the alley, she got a good slash on his upper arm, and he let go. Kipper fell backward into the dirt and was scrambling to run away when Trudith came bounding to her side.

"Want to play?" Trudith asked and shoved a scramball in her face.

Kipper scrabbled back to her feet, smoothing her fur and recollecting her dignity. "No," she said, breathless and confused. "We have to go."

"Aw come on," Trudith said, completely unaware of Kipper's recent fright.

The other dogs, now clearly an impromptu, ragtag scramball team, gathered around and joined in Trudith's cajoling. Most of the dogs were Chihuahuas and Xolos. Kipper couldn't make out their words, but she got the idea that they felt better matched to her than Trudith.

"If you play one game," Trudith said, making her final offer, "I'll buy you dinner when we get to Guatemala."

Given that Kipper wouldn't have access to Alistair's wired funds until they hit Ecuador, she couldn't afford to turn down a free dinner. Also, if they stopped at a restaurant, she might be able to pick out something easier on the stomach than Trudith's choice of car snacks. Kipper put her paws out to accept the scramball.

Kipper had never played the game before, but she couldn't have worked in an office environment with dogs for as long as she had without picking up the basics. It helped that these dogs seemed to be playing by looser rules than usual.

The twenty-odd dogs were divided unevenly into three teams. Trudith's team was the smallest, and Kipper's the largest, to make up for their disparate abilities. At any given time, one team had the ball and was trying to get it to the second team. The third team was trying to steal it. If Team One got the ball to Team Two, then both teams scored. Then Team Two took over trying to get the ball to Team Three, and Team One had to try to steal it.

However, if Teams One and Two failed, and Team Three stole the ball, then Team Three got double points. And, then, the order would reverse.

From Kipper's perspective, there were suddenly a lot of dogs to dodge, swipe (with sheathed claws), and duck between. The ball itself was a highly theoretical object, lost somewhere among the sea of dogs on the yellow team. Her own team—defined as "the dogs in green plus the cat"—was fanned out around the main fray.

A huge cheer rose from her team when a Chihuaua sporting a yellow bandana on his arm managed to pass the ball through the ring of red team blockers. The entire topology of the field changed with the passing of the ball. Red team dogs found themselves shoved bodily away from anyone wearing a speck of green. And vice versa. Kipper decided her goal would be to keep from getting the wind knocked out of her. She ducked and weaved among the dogs in red, mostly trying to keep their big paws off of her.

Her plan backfired, however, when one of her teammates, a hairless, black-skinned Xolo dog, got the ball. "Hey, cat!" he called. "You're good at dodging! Can you catch?"

Kipper hadn't meant to impress anyone. And she certainly hadn't meant to end up with the ball. There was only a split second to decide though, and she didn't want to be "that hilariously pathetic cat who ran from the ball." So, instead of becoming a laughingstock, Kipper threw out her paws. The ball slammed her in the chest, knocking the wind out of her, but she wrapped her arms tight around it. Then she took off running before the entire field of dogs could converge, violently, on the spot.

Barreling forward, dodging erratically, Kipper realized she needed a plan. She had to keep the ball away from yellow, and get it to someone—*anyone*—wearing something green or red. Fortunately, she was good at thinking on her feet. Or so she'd thought before playing scramball...

Running and dodging bought her time, but she could only run for so long. The only dogs that even got near her all wore telltale scraps of yellow. Bandanas tied around necks or arms; a ratty t-shirt. Trudith sported a yellow sash, borrowed and tied around her middle. About to give up, Kipper had an idea. She aimed straight for Trudith, leaping with all her cat's might. Dogs are strong and fast, but they can't jump like cats.

Kipper sailed right over Trudith, landing on her surprised companion's back. Holding on tight with her legs and one arm,

Kipper waved the scramball in the air, furiously searching the mosh of dogs for a teammate who was clear.

When she finally divested herself of the ball, Kipper slid down Trudith's back, and sank to the ground. But she didn't stay there long before getting back in the game. To her utter surprise, Kipper's small size and limber agility counted for almost as much as the dog players' weight. She was *good* at scramball.

Exhilarated and exhausted by the end of the game, Kipper crashed against Trudith's side for support, panting like one of the dogs. "That was fun," she said. "I've got to start up a scramball team for cats when this is all done."

"There are already a few," Trudith said, bouncing the scramball back to a lanky Xolo.

One of the Chihuahua's from Kipper's team came up to her and shook her paws, speaking a few indecipherable words. She guessed he was congratulating her on the game. Then, he looked her over and pulled off his green scramball jersey, holding it out for her. Most of the dogs didn't have real jerseys, but this Chihuahua had a real, numbered scramball jersey.

"Take it," Trudith said. "It'll fit you."

Kipper grinned and threw the green jersey on over her blue tunic. It was number twenty-five, and she decided that would be her new lucky number. She'd never felt more accepted. "Thank you," she said, giving the Chihuahua a hug. "Really, thanks."

Chapter 6

The next few days were a blur of countries outside Kipper's window.

Guatemala became El Salvador and then Honduras. The terrain grew mountainous, green, and jungly. Wild rainforests alternated with farmland, growing sugarcane and coffee beans. Kipper slept through Nicaragua and most of Costa Rica, but she took the wheel through all of Panama and down into Colombia. South America at last!

The air got hotter and wetter. As they worked their way south, the humidity was on the rise. The moistness in the air stuck Kipper's fur against her, and she shed her long-sleeved tunic. The scramball jersey was infinitely cooler and more comfortable, even if it did show her naturally tabby shoulders and upper arms. She was getting used to the indignity; it was better than broiling inside her tunic.

When Trudith was awake, they talked about scramball, Moonville Funpark, and whether Senator Morrison would get his law passed that banned cats in space. When Trudith slept and Kipper drove, she speculated about Sahalie's nefarious dealings with underhanded dogs and tried to riddle out Violet's scribbled notes. Unfortunately, she couldn't get very far on her own. She'd have to wait until she got to the space elevator, where hopefully she'd find Petra. Then the two of them could ride it together, all the way up to otter space and find Violet who could explain everything.

Kipper strained her eyes, but she couldn't see the twin ribbons of the space elevator yet. Even as they drove down the streets of Guayaquil, the biggest city in Ecuador and largest port-town in the world, she couldn't make out a double line parting the sky, rising into the void.

"I thought it would look like a cloud trail left by a jet," she said, trying not to sound too disappointed.

"You can't see it until you get very close. The ribbons are thin down here," Trudith said as she parked their car near the docks. Shrimp boats, cruise ships headed for the Galapagos, and every other manner of sea vehicle crowded the bay, bobbing lazily in the water. Kipper smelled shrimp and shellfish in the tangy sea air.

"Are you coming with me to the elevator?" Kipper asked.

Trudith shrugged, "I've come this far, and I wouldn't want to hear later that Sahalie sent thugs to wait for you there. If she sends thugs, then you should have thugs. And that's me."

Kipper grinned. "Every cat should have her own thug. Tell you what, I'll go get my money and call Alistair. You pick up tickets for the ferry to the elevator landing."

Trudith had been so generous. She always paid for charging the car, keeping it stocked in snacks, and she'd bought Kipper nice restaurant dinners several times. It would feel good to be able to pay her back, even if only a little. There was no way that Kipper could pay for all the time Trudith had given her.

Before leaving the car, Kipper pulled on one of her long-sleeved tunics to wear under her scramball jersey. The sea air was slightly chill, and she felt more embarrassed by her fur in such a big, international city.

Guayaquil was an animal city the way animal cities were *meant* to be. Sure, there were still human buildings, but they were breathtaking, historical monuments. Towering cathedrals and columnated government buildings had been preserved in mint condition and were mostly used as museums now. However, unlike New LA and Mexico City, there were no crumbling ruins. The streets were all new, and the animal buildings were geometrically organized. They made up the bulk of the city, rather than crouching in between human wreckage, forced to fit inside the antiquated human layout.

And there were otters everywhere! Sure there were dogs of every breed, wearing loud, flowered vests, with cameras hung around their necks. There were even cats; one had a broom and was sweeping out a shop as Kipper passed. Yet, here was one of the only cities in the world with a significant population of otters.

Kipper thrilled to see them pass by. Their long bodies bobbed and swayed as they walked; their short legs as compared to their long backs made them move completely differently from dogs and cats. She'd only seen otters on the news before. It was completely different in person.

Just outside the Coastal Canine Bank, Kipper found a pay-vidphone and dialed her brother. She twitched her tail impatiently as the phone rang. She wanted to share her excitement with her brother. Five rings, and he didn't answer. Eventually, the message machine picked up, but Kipper didn't dare to leave a message. She'd worked herself up too much over the last few days, thinking about Sahalie for hours on end. It was paranoid, and she knew it.

Yet, she didn't know if she'd be able to call Alistair easily from space (there would probably be exorbitant space to Earth charges), so she tried again. With a heavy heart, Kipper had to admit by the third try that he simply wasn't in. She hoped he wasn't in some sort of trouble.

Inside the Coastal Canine Bank, Kipper waited in line. It was sad, not knowing when she'd hear from her brother again. When she got to the teller window, she told the dog there her assumed name—Mother Theresa B. Goodkitty. She got a strange look, but the dog went to the back room, rustled around a bit, and returned with an envelope for her. She thanked him.

Walking back to the docks, Kipper ripped open the edge of the envelope and leafed through the bills inside. She divided them approximately evenly—half to pay back Trudith and the other half to keep. That much money should keep her—and Petra—for a while. She slipped her half back in the envelope, folded it over, and slipped it inside an inner tunic pocket, beneath her scramball jersey. There it would be safe from the wind, her carelessness, and any but the most skillful and determined pickpockets.

Then, Kipper opened the smaller envelope that had been paper-clipped to it. Encouraging words, she figured, from her brother when he wired the money. Yet, she had to read the first sentence several times. It didn't make sense. "I'm in jail," it said. Kipper checked the date, and she realized the note had been attached to the envelope with the money only yesterday. She read the note again, and this time it made more sense.

"I'm in jail," Alistair wrote, "but don't worry about it. It's the best thing that could happen. The cats are rallying in the streets for me, and my fellow jailbirds are all taking my side. Even the dogs! They know what it's like to be repressed by The Man—*The Dog*—too. Pin down that conspiracy for me, and we'll run for president. Felines for Freedom! —Cheers, Alistair."

Kipper's eyes grew wide, and she laughed like a kitten. Her brother was showing a new side.

Back at the car, Trudith was leaning into the trunk, emptying one of her smaller luggage bags. When she'd moved everything out of the purple duffle, she put in the few changes of clothes she'd bought for Kipper. She also stuffed in the rest of the snacks.

"Here," she said, when she heard Kipper arrive. "You'll need a suitcase for traveling, so I gave you one of mine."

Kipper took the little, purple duffel bag in her paws. She was deeply touched. "Trudith... Where will you go once I'm on the elevator?"

Trudith's ears went back in that stricken look that made her jowly face gaunt. Her brown eyebrows peaked in confusion. "I don't know..." she said. "I can't work for Sahalie any more... Maybe I should come with you?"

"No, I think I have to follow this trail alone." Trudith had become like a surrogate sister on this trip, but Kipper was about to find and rejoin her own sister. And she figured the two of them would have a better chance finding Violet on their own. Two cats looking for a lone cat. A big, scary dog would just get in the way.

But, from Trudith's face, Kipper realized that the dog had probably been planning to accompany her as far as this road led. It would be a kindness to tell Trudith what she should do. She needed a task.

"Would you do something for me?" Kipper asked. "Alistair's in jail..." As funny as it was, Kipper felt a twinge of fear actually saying the words. Alistair didn't belong behind bars any more than a fluffy little gerbil did. "Could you go back to New LA? And help him out?"

"Your brother's in jail?" Trudith asked, her gruff voice forceful with an emotion between outrage for the undercat, who was apparently her new poorly-paying employer, and enthusiasm for a new job. "The Alistair you've told me about? Why would anyone want to throw a stand-up cat like him in jail?"

Kipper knew it would be unkind to remind Trudith of their original relationship, but Trudith must have thought of it herself. Her big, brown eyes rolled downward, avoiding Kipper's gaze. She clearly still felt guilty.

"Could you go help him?" Kipper asked. "I'd feel better if he had a dog like you looking out for him. A sort of bodyguard."

"Or assistant! Secretary to the District Rep!"

"Yeah, something like that," Kipper said, realizing how much she would miss this big, dumb dog.

The two of them talked it over and agreed that it would be best if Trudith took the next flight out. She knew a dog here who could sell her car for her, and it would be faster to fly. With difficulty, Kipper convinced Trudith to take her money. It was only fair, she argued, that she pay for her half of the car charges and road food. Besides, if Trudith really objected, she could apply the money to helping Alistair.

The final goodbye was rough and sloppy. First a hug that jolted Kipper out of balance, and then a wet kiss on either cheek. Trudith's brown eyes embraced Kipper as well. The look in them said, "you're my cat," and it was a kind of ownership that went both ways. Because Trudith felt Kipper belonged to her, Trudith wholly belonged to Kipper. If only Trudith could have skipped the slobbery kisses, it would have been a perfect goodbye.

Trudith wasn't a bad dog; she just needed a little guidance. Alistair, on the other paw, could be a reckless fool. He *was* Petra's brother. He needed protection, and he needed it bad. The two would do well in each others' paws.

And so Kipper, purple duffle slung over her shoulder, boarded the ferry to the space elevator alone. She kept her long-sleeved tunic buttoned up high, and she even put in the blue contacts. Not all blue-eyed white cats are deaf, but enough are that it would give her the element of surprise. Just in case she needed it.

On board the boat, Kipper used her disguise to move freely among the other passengers, listening in. As far as she could tell, she was the only cat on board for the forty minute ride. There were tourist dogs with their puppies, hyped up on sugar and the idea of Moonville Funpark rides, and there were sharply-dressed business otters by the dozen.

One pair of otters noticed her approach, but since they assumed she couldn't hear they took the opportunity to begin talking about cats. Kipper was pleased to find that she understood their accents perfectly from all the otter news she'd watched.

"Have you heard about the dogs in the U.S.?" the first otter asked. He was a sleek, chic, and sinewy river otter.

The second otter, a puffy but dapper sea otter, patted himself down, searching his pockets until he found a tin of clam chews. "What about them?" he asked, popping one of the treats into his mouth. The river otter deferred when the sea otter offered the tin to him, and so the sea otter swung around and offered the tin to Kipper, sitting in a row of seats off to their side. He pointed at the lid of the tin but didn't bother to speak. Kipper took a chew and smiled. She bobbed her ears in a motion of thanks but didn't break her disguise.

"I say, you haven't heard then. They're trying to ban cats from entering space."

"That's outrageous!" the sea otter proclaimed.

Kipper almost choked on the clam chew, breaking her disguise, but she covered her surprise by unzipping her duffle bag and rustling around inside. She could feel the sea otter looking at her. What did he mean by what he'd said? Were the otters on the cats' side?

"It's this Senator Morisson bloke," the river otter continued. "He's been pushing it for the last year."

"You know, it seems to me that dogs have gotten a little too comfortable on Earth. Do you think we should start a war with them?"

"It would be good fun," the river otter said. "But I don't think it will come to that. The dogs don't own the elevator," he shrugged, "so there's not much they can do if we let cats on." Kipper felt an immense sense of relief. Senator Morisson's pending law had been the bane of any forward thinking cats' existence for the last year.

Yet, with only a few words, the otters had dispelled the law's power. In Kipper's eyes, anyway. *Senator Morisson couldn't keep cats like her from space... How had she not known?* Living in a dog run world, she had accepted the dogs' own estimation of their importance. And power. But... Dogs didn't really run the world. At least not all of it.

"Too true. Too true," the sea otter said, rising from his seat. "Let's take a stroll on the outer deck, shall we? Feel that honest sea breeze before getting back to the rivers in the sky." He smiled down at Kipper, poor deaf cat, before tottering on.

Kipper liked that phrase: *rivers in the sky.* Otters were so sophisticated and true romantics. Not like dogs. Nothing against Trudith—Kipper had grown quite fond of her during the last week, but she was such a simpleton compared to otters. Let the dogs have Earth. Cats belonged with otters in the *rivers in the sky.* Well, at least, the sky. She could do without most rivers, but what cat didn't enjoy a good metaphor?

When the ferry docked, dogs and otters filed off the boat and onto the monstrous sea structure that was the *elevator platform.*

The platform itself was a broad, steel structure floating on the calm of the sea. It was large enough and solid enough that it gave the illusion of being rooted to ground underneath the water. Wavelets lapped against its sides, and buildings clustered around its edges, including restaurants, gift shops, and other tourist destinations.

However, the heart of the platform was the open, landing area in the center for the *climbers*—the elevator cars. Out of that area rose two thin strands of woven carbon nano-tubes. These cables were what the climbers climbed. Kipper thrilled to see the climbers there, folded around the carbon cables like spiders dangling from silken thread. One carbon cable was empty, rising into the sky as lonely as a shed whisker. But, three climbers were stacked, one atop another, at the bottom of the other cable. When they began to climb, the climbers at the top of the other cable would begin to descend.

As Kipper stared at the wonder of construction and technology around her, feeling the paradoxical solidity and levity under her feet, she felt her heart begin to sink inside her. It wasn't reasonable or rational, but she had expected to step one paw on the platform island and find Petra waiting for her. Orange-striped arms and an acerbic tongue would greet her. And two sister-cats would crack wide open the conspiracy surrounding Sahalie and Violet. Then they would paint space red.

Instead, Kipper found herself standing alone, surrounded by tourdogs and business-otters she didn't know. She had to face the reality of the fact that Petra, traveling alone, either made it onto an airplane before Sahalie could send a second round of dogs after her—meaning she would have arrived days ago—or, she had a drive that would take twice as long with half the drivers.

Deep down, Kipper felt that Petra had to be ahead of her. She'd left first, and she wouldn't think twice about dangers like running into another group of thug-dogs at airport security. She was the impulsive type...

Either way though, Kipper, honestly, had no idea how to find her. Would Petra wait on the platform for her? Kipper looked around. It would be easy enough to skulk around the tourist shops and spots, waiting for her sister to catch up with her. But did Petra even expect Kipper to be following her? And... Well... Kipper knew Petra. Even if she did understand that Kipper had to follow that note she left, "*Gone to Ecuador!*", she wasn't big on patience. And even Kipper could feel the impossible pull of those elevators, begging her to step inside, ride up to space, and taste a new kind of freedom. If Kipper was even a *little* swayed by that pull, Petra would give right in. Impulsive type, remember?

So, feeling a little hurt and angry—reasonably or not—that her quest hadn't rejoined her with her sister yet, Kipper stepped into the line for elevator tickets. She hoped that Petra would be easy to find on space-side.

As the line advanced, Kipper pulled the envelope out of her tunic and looked up at the signboard posting the prices. She gulped. How could this be?! She'd been saving money for her whole life, and she wouldn't have had a *fraction* of the cost of a lousy *one-way* ticket into space, even if Alistair had wired *everything she had.*

The business-otters and tourdogs in line with her didn't even look at the signboard with ticket prices; they handed over plastic and paid the exorbitant sums. Not a blink of a canine eye. So much for that sea otter's grand ideals about otters subverting the dogs' plans to ban cats from space. At least the dogs were honest about it. The otters were hiding behind a price tag.

Kipper spat at the otters in line. She spat at the dogs next. She spat at the ticket stand. And, she spat at the unfairness of a world where a dog was paid big bucks to beat her up, and she was paid a pitiful pittance for doing honest, hard work.

Kipper glared at the dogs in the line, subconsciously looking for a Chow, hoping to pick a fight. Lucky for her, there were no Chows going to Moonville Funpark that day. Even in her red rage, Kipper knew that picking a fight was more likely to get her thrown in a Guayaquil jail than into space. And it would be a while before Trudith could come and rescue her.

Kipper pulled the increasingly crumpled note that had started this whole mess from her tunic pocket. If Petra and Violet had made it onto the space elevator before her then there had to be a way.

"@ SE, ask for Chip—night flight."

Huh. Suddenly that part wasn't cryptic any more. Kipper stepped out of the futile line and walked up to the first otter she could find. "Do you know Chip?" she asked. It broke her cover, but pretending to be deaf wasn't really doing her much good.

The otter pointed her toward the actual base of the space elevator, where huge crates were being loaded by forklift into the cargo hold of the bottom most climber. "Thanks," Kipper said, and took off that way.

The only creature amid the bustle ahead of her, who wasn't driving a forklift, was a short, officious looking, bearded Jack Russell with a clipboard. Kipper had been hoping for another otter. This mini-goon didn't look like a gateway to otter space, let alone Cat Havana, but he did look like he might be a "Chip." He would have to do.

"Chip?" Kipper asked, skeptically.

"Yes?" the dog asked. "I'm very busy." His eyes barely even flitted away from the clipboard to look at her. In fact, his grip on the clipboard seemed to tighten as Kipper approached.

She really had been hoping for an otter. Oh well. She'd asked for "Chip," and she'd got him. Now it was time for step two. "I was hoping to get a..." Kipper was careful to put extra emphasis on the next words, "*night flight.*"

For that, Chip looked up. The clipboard was still clutched tightly in his paws, but his eyes took Petra in, looking her up and down. To him, she was just a scruffy-lookin' cat, about his height, but wispier. Chip was built like a barrel—solid chested with medium length legs and arms. Chip narrowed his eyes at her. "You don't look like the others..."

Kipper instinctively, defensively responded, "I had to dye my fur." Of course, then the strangeness of Chip's words hit her... However, her words didn't seem to be strange to him at all.

"Oh, okay," Chip said. He gazed hard into Kipper's clear blue eyes. "Yeah, okay. I wasn't expecting you, but I'll add it to the growing tab."

Growing tab... Did that mean Kipper wasn't the first unexpected cat? Had Petra already passed this way? Looking at Chip, grumpily flipping through the pages on his clipboard, Kipper was afraid to ask. But, at least she knew *some* other cats had been through here. Hopefully, Petra was one of them.

Chip found the page he was looking for, and noted something down with his pen. Grumbling, he said, "Sahalie needs to start keeping better records..."

The words—*that name*—sent a shock through Kipper's body. What was Sahalie playing at? As an accountant, probably embezzlement. But, why would she use her ill-gotten funds to buy some cats space elevator tickets and other cats one-way tickets to the morgue?

Kipper was knocked out of her reverie, and almost off her feet, by a crate-loaded dolly. Chip, clipboard tucked under his arm, had wheeled the thing right into her. "Here's how it works," he said. "I can put you on the *night flight* as the custodian of the live squid shipment. Someone has to watch the tank, and no one will notice if you slip away once you're up top. So, just don't come back down. This is a one way ride."

Kipper nodded, wrestling to keep the heavy dolly upright. It seemed to have a wonky wheel.

"Until then, I need you to work. Load cargo from there," Chip gestured at a depressingly large pile of crates and trunks, "to there." Following Chip's second gesture, Kipper peered into the dark, cavernous hold of the bottom crawler. If the live squid shipment was somewhere in there, she guessed she would miss the view on the ride up. Oh well. That was better than missing the ride.

Chapter 7

Chip was a harsh task-master. He kept Kipper lugging crates of shrimp, tanks of crabs, and other sea-farmed delectables along with trunk after trunk of passenger luggage until her agile cat-spine ached. Cats weren't built for hard work, and this work was back-breaking.

She loaded cargo until the climbers took off. She watched the dogs and otters who had ridden the ferry with her ascend into the sky. Even though they took the climbers with them, Chip managed to find more tasks for Kipper. He kept her busy unloading cargo from ocean-barges, arranging it on the elevator platform to wait for the climbers on the other cable to finish their descent.

Kipper was run ragged by the time the climbers actually arrived, loaded with cargo. She wished she had Trudith with her to help unload it. Or maybe the whole Mexican scramball team... They'd make short work out of a long job for her. It was a comfort wearing her jersey.

In fact the work kept her hot enough from exertion that Kipper stripped off her long-sleeved tunic and stuffed it in her purple duffel. It was a relief to have her arms bared to the tropical air. The warm breeze stirred her fur which had been smashed, damp, and sweltering in the tunic. Sure, the jersey showed the gray stripes on her shoulders, but if she was playing the part of heavy-labor, she saw no reason to look the part of an aristocat. Besides, none of the elevator passengers were coming anywhere near the cargo entrance to the climber. They stayed on the touristy half of the island. So, the only animal likely to see her was Chip, and he already knew she'd dyed her fur.

On and off she loaded luggage, barely getting breaks between one climber taking off and the next arriving. Descend, ascend. Unload, reload. Kipper had become a part of the space elevator machinery.

The sky slowly darkened, and the equatorial air grew a few degrees cooler. Kipper could feel the approach of her "night flight." She peered into the sky and searched for a pinpoint of light that might be a climber coming to whisk her away.

"The next one will be your ride," Chip said, calling to her from across the platform. "So, get it loaded fast, and we'll be done for the night."

Before she looked back up, Kipper could already hear the grumbling approach of the climbers. When she looked up, the mammoth elevator cars were blotting out the stars in the sky. The air around her lifted in a wind as the climber flashed its landing lights. She got straight to work, and, despite her aching, wobbly muscles, had the climber loaded in record time.

Chip stomped over and checked her work. He sniffed and wiped his wet nose with a poorly manicured paw. "Are you ready, cat, to watch those squid?"

"Aye!" Kipper answered, with more enthusiasm than was really called for by squid baby-sitting. Chip gave her a suspicious look, and Kipper could see the red in his eyes. Then, he stomped off, gesturing for Kipper to follow him.

He led her to a locked shed, opened it, and began wheeling the giant, sloshing squid tank that was inside backward and into a sharp turn, aiming it for the climber.

"Here, cat," Chip said and stepped away, handing control over to her. "These are expensive. A delicacy up there. So take good care of them."

Kipper nodded as she began struggling with the tank. Chip might be about her size, but he was clearly a lot stronger. He peered at her strangely in the dim light, but Kipper was more concerned with keeping the tank squarely on its dolly than with the stare of a strange dog. Thankfully, this dolly wasn't the one with the wonky wheel.

Chip clucked his tongue, watching her. He made no motion to help, standing back as Kipper shoved at the wheeled but hard to budge tank. "I thought you dyed your fur," he said, narrowing his eyes.

"I did," Kipper huffed between shoves.

"But, why would you dye your shoulders like that?"

"What?" Kipper looked down at her shoulders, despite knowing what they looked like. "No, that's my natural color." Kipper could feel the strain in her muscles rising through her body into a dizzy headache between her ears. Seeing that Chip was still watching her expectantly, she added "I dyed the rest white." Hopefully that would send the butch little task-master on his way.

Chip simply said, "Oh...", wheels turning in his beady-eyed head. Then, "I thought you were Siamese."

Kipper laughed, a manic laugh bred from tension, but refrained from giving Chip the speech about the difference between true and bottle-job Siamese. She didn't have the extra breath if she was going to get the tank of squid to where it needed to be. Besides, she felt less high and mighty about it now, with her arms and head a frazzled, chemically bleached white.

Finally, the Jack Russell walked away, pawing his tiny beard. Kipper kept wrestling with the squid tank until she got it positioned safely past the yellow safety line painted on the concrete floor of the climber.

She could sense the tension in the machinery of the climber, all the gears hidden inside its walls, as it readied to climb. The slight vibration in the miles long carbon cable, streaming upward into the dark, rose in pitch as the climber gripped it, raising her spirits with it. Kipper grinned in tired relief. The long day of work was over. She grabbed her purple duffel from where she'd stowed it and went to tell Chip she was done.

Chip was twenty feet away in his ticket station. Kipper brushed her paws off on her jersey as she approached. Through the glass over the ticketing counter, she could see Chip dialing numbers into the vidphone on the back wall. She stopped just short of knocking on the glass. The vidphone had crackled into an open channel, and she didn't want to disturb Chip in the middle of a call.

A moment later, Kipper was glad she'd waited. She could just make out the face on the vidscreen: fine gray stripes and clear blue eyes. *Sahalie.*

It didn't take a whole thought, let alone a second one, to realize that Sahalie would give her away. Chip would soon be looking for her and an explanation. If she was lucky. If not, he'd just be looking for her. Like Trudith had been. Way back when.

Even if Chip was planning to listen to her, she didn't think she could talk herself out of this one. Chip was clearly Sahalie's dog, and Sahalie had already shown her what she liked to do with her dogs. Not every one of them could turn out to be a Trudith. And Chip didn't seem much like Trudith. Kipper didn't wait to find out.

She dropped to all fours and pelted across the tarmac between her and the invitingly dark nooks and crannies inside the loaded elevator climber. She spanned the distance to the cargo hold before Chip was even off the phone.

A frantic look around the dark cavern of the climber's hold left Kipper with sagging ears. She'd put all of these crates here. And all of them were heavy. And none of them were easy to open—most of them looking like they were designed to be torn apart by crowbar. Glancing back over her shoulder, she could see Chip emerging from the ticket station. He disappeared in the direction of the dock. That meant he was going for reinforcements. Kipper *had* to get herself hidden.

She decided her best bet was a configuration of crates near the back of the hold. A beam jutting out from the wall, a little higher than the top of the crates, would provide some shelter from above, if she could get herself ensconced behind them.

Her heart racing and her arms shaking, Kipper jostled the boxes along the wall to find one light enough to move without the dolly. The winning contestant was a crate marked "Paris Poodle Pastries." Although the pastries made for the lightest crate in the row, they were still heavy enough to belie their ever-catchy advertising campaign: they were *not* lighter than air.

Kipper shimmied the wooden pastry crate far enough away from the crates around it to squeeze in behind. Once there, she kicked and heaved against the other crates until their haphazard angles afforded her a hidden cove large enough to crouch inside. Fortunately, she had packed all of the crates somewhat haphazardly, so the change wouldn't be immediately obvious.

From her crouch, Kipper reached one paw around the corner of the pastry crate, dug her claws in, braced herself with her other paw, and yanked until the entryway closed. She twisted around, positioning the purple duffel like a pillow behind her back and focused on steadying her breathing.

Gruff dog voices preceded the plodding sound of dog paws. "A stowaway?" one voice, unfamiliar, was saying. From the easy lilt, Kipper guessed the speaker was a Golden. At least, she was pretty sure the speaker wasn't a Basset—thank goodness, or she'd certainly be found.

"A cat," Chip said. "A funny white and gray one. I saw it come running back here."

"I didn't see any cats arrive on the last boat," the possibly-Golden said.

"It musta been hangin' around since earlier today."

"Why didn't it stow away earlier?"

There was an uncomfortable pause. Kipper could hear the two dogs shifting boxes on the other side of the hold, and she could feel slivers stinging her paw pads. She must have got them from moving the wooden crates, but she didn't dare try doctoring her paws now. She didn't dare move. She hardly dared breath.

"Look, Chip," said the Golden—Kipper was sure he must be a Golden by now, because she was banking everything on the legendary affability and easygoing nature of that breed. When they found her—and they were so near her now, they had to find her—a Golden *probably* wouldn't rough her up. "Look, I know you've got this side deal going with smuggling the Siamese cats up the elevator..." The voice was coming from just the other side of Kipper's pastry box. "... and I look the other way. We all do. But..." The pastry box creaked; Kipper guessed the Golden must be leaning against it. "See, you can't be letting these cats cause problems like this all the time. I mean, we have a schedule to keep."

Kipper could hear a growl that must have been coming from deep in Chip's voice box. "Fine!" he barked as the box jumped, squeezing Kipper tighter, probably in response to a swift kick. That Jack Russell might be short, but Kipper sure wouldn't want to fight with him.

"Look, I'll radio the otters up top, and they can have the authorities pick this cat up."

"No, never mind it," Chip said. "I'll call some goons up; deal with it myself. Don't tell the swimmers."

"All right. But, the otters are going to find out eventually." The voices were starting to recede now. Kipper could just make out the Golden saying, "You really shouldn't get so mixed up in all this cat nonsense. They'll just make trouble for you. Stowaways... Petty theft... Typical cat stuff."

Typical dog stuff; blame it on the cats. Seriously, petty theft? How was she supposed to commit petty theft with all these boxes nailed shut? Not that she would mind trying one of *Paris Poodles'* famous puff pastries. On the ads, the pictures of the ones filled with crab ragout looked particularly delectable.

Kipper pushed her nose against a crack between the wooden slats to see if she could make out the smell of crab ragout inside. All she could smell was wood. However, her disappointment was short lived. Though she couldn't smell anything she liked, she could hear something she very much liked, a sound she'd heard repeatedly today: the sound of the cargo doors closing.

The final clanking touchdown was followed by an ominous hum. It was the hum of the lights powering down, and Kipper realized she would spend the entire hour and a half flight in the dark. No matter. Her cat's eyes were already adjusting.

Clambering awkwardly from behind the pastry crate, she felt a pang at how little difference she could sense between plummeting upwards into space and, well, *not*. Without windows to show her the Earth shrinking beneath her, or even a noticeable acceleration, the climber might as well still be on the landing pad for all she knew.

She'd read before about how the space elevator was so perfectly designed—with a slowly increasing acceleration for the first half, switching to a slowly increasing *deceleration* for the second half. Passengers didn't feel the slightest discomfort. She'd been impressed by that. But, now—actually riding the elevator—she wished for a little discomfort. Just a little. Just to let her *feel* that it was *real*.

Of course, several extra gees wouldn't really be in Kipper's best interest. She had an hour and a half before Chip's "goons" would come walking in that cargo door. She needed a better hiding place than behind *Paris Poodles*. Maybe one of the crates would be loose enough to open, and she could hide inside? Then, when the crate was unloaded, she'd be carried safely past the goons. That was her best hope. Short of that, she would have to trade invisibility against ease of escape: the better she stacked the boxes around her, the harder it would be to make a break for it when the time came. Or, even, to recognize that the time had come. Assuming one did...

The worst part of being alone in the dark was knowing, now, that there would be no one waiting for her. Petra couldn't have paid for a ticket into space any better than Kipper could. And Kipper realized now that Chip had only helped her because he thought she was Siamese, like Violet. There was no mistaking Petra and her electrically orange stripes for Siamese. So, unless Petra had dyed her fur too—*unlikely*—she wouldn't be at the top of the elevator waiting for Kipper with open arms.

Kipper was still scrabbling at boxes, digging her claws deep into their wooden slats and pulling hard to break off their immovable lids, when the flight hit its midpoint. Her paws felt light on the floor, and her stomach became queasy. She'd seen vids of the space elevator so she figured out what was happening pretty quickly, even though she couldn't see it.

The passenger and cargo carriers, responding to the shift from acceleration to deceleration, were filled with a simulated reversed gravity. The solution to this tricky meeting of engineering and ergonomics? The two holds—passenger and cargo—were attached to the core of the climber by a mechanical rotator cuff. And, one hold balancing the other out, they rotated in opposite directions, resulting in them making the rest of the ascent upside down. Perfectly matching the upside down gravity.

The practical upshot? Kipper felt her paw pads lift off the cold metal floor, and all of her fur puffed out at the eerie sensation of being surrounded by dozens of heavy cargo crates that had moved so imperceptibly she could barely see it with her cat eye vision in the darkness. And, yet, she could sense they were floating. *Spooky.*

A moment later, everything in the hold silently landed. The crates hadn't risen high enough above the ground to create air gaps large enough for noisy crashes.

Kipper wondered what would happen at the end of the flight when the holds disconnected from the climbing apparatus of the climber so they could be shifted from the center to the outer edge of the rotating, tubular donut that was Deep Sky Anchor station. During that process, there would be a whole minute of weightlessness. If not several. Kipper could explore the ceiling of the hold if she wanted. Actually... That gave Kipper an idea.

Craning her neck back, Kipper edged around the hold, examining the dimly visible, distant ceiling. There were pipes, and machinery, up there. Even with her night-vision cat's eyes, the details were lost to her in the gloom. Nonetheless, she now had a plan.

With nothing to do to further her plan until the last minutes of the flight, Kipper was sorely tempted to catch a brief nap. The floor was hard and uncomfortable, but the hold was dark and quiet. And cats need their naps. However, Kipper couldn't risk missing the brief window she'd have for effecting her plan, so she had to settle for one of those alert drowses that dogs often mistake for real naps. It's not like real sleep, though. Any cat knows the difference.

The decreasing acceleration was so gradual that, despite Kipper's alertness, she didn't notice she was practically floating until she felt the thunderous *kachunk* that must have been the crawling apparatus inside the climber disengaging from the carbon cord. She immediately jumped into action. Literally. And, underestimating her new lightness, the impetus of her jump hurled her all the way to the high, high ceiling of the hold and—*crash*—resoundingly into it.

If she'd been made out of rubber, she would have bounced all the way back to the floor. Instead, she just bruised her back and shoulders. And hung there. Her back was against the ceiling, but she wasn't lying on it. She was just hovering there, looking down at the entire hold, yawning beneath her. Her perspective kept flipping, as if she were looking at one of those optical illusion sketches where if you look at it one way it's a silly looking dog with its tongue hanging out, but, then, suddenly, it'll be two cats playing checkers.

Well, one moment, the room had flipped upside down and she was lying on the ceiling; then, suddenly, the room would be right side up again and she just *knew* that she would fall any moment.

Of course, if she waited long enough, the climber would finish its lateral trip to the rotating edge of Deep Sky Anchor, and gravity would return. Then she really *would* fall.

So, Kipper pulled herself together, checked that the straps of her duffel were still over her shoulder (she could no longer feel the pull of the duffel's weight, since it now had none), and gave a gentle push against the ceiling behind her. The right-pawed push twisted her around to where the ceiling was underneath her. Her new floor. Moving was less dizzying that way.

Awkwardly, she scrabbled along the ceiling, digging her claws into seams between metal panels, and gripping pipes as she came by them, to keep from drifting uselessly away from the ceiling, toward the real floor.

By the time the crawler *kathunk*ed, summoning the return of gravity, Kipper was ready for it. In every way.

She was perched on top of a nexus of pipes above the entry hatch to the crawler: the perfect place to watch Chip's goons search for her; herself, searching for an opportunity to escape. But, also, she was ready to feel lithe and agile again. Which she simply didn't in zero gee. Her vast inexperience with zero gee made her feel awkward and... uncatlike.

But, most importantly, she was ready to get out of this elevator. Then she'd be *in space*. Something she'd hitherto only dreamed about. And even though none of her dreams had been anything like this, stepping onto that space station would still be a triumph. She'd figure out the next stage of her crazy journey from there.

Chapter 8

The door opened, spilling space station light into the hold. Kipper could hardly wait to set paw on the light-kissed ground. The closer she got to otter space, the more buzzed she got. She wanted to get out there and see what Deep Sky Anchor was really like. She wanted to join the otters, swimming in their "rivers in the sky."

The only thing between her and those "rivers" were a squat, white bulldog and the lanky-lookin' bloodhound nosing around the elevator entrance. Chip's goons. She could tell them apart from the hired hands—also dogs—because they weren't wheeling dollies into the hold. No, their paws were free. And their eyes, ears, and noses were searching.

Kipper was particularly worried by the bloodhound's nose. Black and moist; twitching ten feet below her. Thank goodness—and the otters who designed the station—that this cargo hold was so tall.

Kipper watched as the bloodhound crouched closer to the floor. The white bulldog, a female, stood beside him. They were both jowly dogs, the tall, red male and the short, white female. Folds of skin flapped all over each of their bodies. There was so much extra skin on the two of them, that Kipper could have folded the excess around herself, making a dog-costume to hide her. And there would have still been enough left that the skin-donors could hardly have missed it.

"Over this way, Luce," the bloodhound barked to his partner.

Luce snarled—or maybe that was just the normal shape of her

face? Kipper couldn't tell. At any rate, the bloodhound followed the scent he'd picked up. It led him back towards the Paris Poodles' crate. Luce, the bulldog, strutted after him, charging toward a random crate here or there, as if to give a phantom cat-in-hiding a scare. Kipper imagined the routine would have worked on her if she'd been behind any of the boxes. Safely above the dogs' heads, however, it just gave her the shivers, fluffing her fur a little.

Kipper tensed and relaxed her claws, compulsively sheathing and unsheathing them, counting out the seconds as Chip's goons moved further and further away from her. The Paris Poodle's crate was in the very back of the hold; so, when they reached it, they'd be as far from her as they would get. After that, her scent trail would just bring them closer. Now was the time. The time to leap and run and get away.

With only the briefest glance at the dogs loading crates on their dollies, Kipper eased herself off of the ceiling pipes and dropped to the floor. So far so good: none of the dogs had seen her, and her landing had been silent. So, they didn't hear her either.

Kipper flattened her body into a crouch; her stomach was barely a centimeter above the floor. She moved herself, slinking, toward the nearest stack of crates. Now that she was safely down, she didn't want to bring attention to herself with any sudden movements. But it was hard: she wanted away from those goons, and she wanted to be out *there*. She wanted to look through a window and see herself surrounded by stars. She wanted to see a world where otters walked around, the proud owners. Instead of dogs. It wasn't cats, but, hey, at least it wasn't dogs.

Now that would be a thing to see. A world owned by cats. The world Petra was looking for. Kipper let out a sigh. She didn't think the dogs could have heard her. The bloodhound was still busy sniffing every corner of the Paris Poodle's crate, but Luce looked around suddenly. "There!" she growled, deep and guttural. The bloodhound snapped his head around, so that his snuffling nose was pointing right at Kipper, folds of jowl pulled into a scowl. Had he seen her? *Yes, he had.*

Every muscle in Kipper's body tensed at once, launching her into the air. For a moment, she hovered there, every fur, dyed or natural on her body sticking straight out. A gray and white puffball, dressed in a green jersey.

Then, almost faster than Chip's goons could see, Kipper twisted her spine around, hit the floor, and was off running into the wild, gray yonder. Steel arches and hatchways were the order of the day, with piles of crates and barrels strewn between them. Kipper dodged between the blue plastic barrels and wooden crates, cutting close to them, hoping to obscure her pursuer's view of her. She was tempted to hide among the cargo, but the bloodhound would sniff her out. No, she needed a way out of Deep Sky Anchor's loading dock. And, she needed a way to divert the bloodhound's nosy nose while she took it.

She stopped to breathe behind one of the giant blue barrels. She was panting like a dog, but a quick glance around the edge of the barrel told her that she hadn't been running like one. She'd been running much faster and was safely, for the moment, out of the goons' sight. She wanted to take a moment and enjoy the feel of space station metal under her feet, but there wasn't time. She had to get her bearings, catch her breath, and plan.

She was leaning against the smooth blue plastic of the barrel, still panting, when she noticed indentations under her paws. The indented words read, "Pure Ganymedean H2O—*Best in the Solar System*." And there was a valve.

Kipper wondered how much damage she could do to the otter's cargo before she became a fugitive of the otters as well as Chip's goons. Well, if she got away fast enough, maybe the otter's would never find out. She imagined the underworld goons and the above board police officials didn't talk to each other much. At least, she hoped not.

Here goes, she thought and threw all her weight into wrenching open the black valve fixture protruding from the giant blue barrel. It resisted at first, but then the water began trickling out. A full turn of the valve, and the water was veritably gushing.

She moved to the next barrel. Soon, the floor was flooded with melted Ganymede, even more gooshing on the way. Kipper wasn't crazy about the feel of Ganymede in the fur between her paw pads. But, it was worth it, if it wiped the track of her scent away. Tiny paw prints—impressions of the oil from her pads—were leading that red furred, baggy skinned nose straight to her. Now, he'd have to be able to scent her through a thin layer of Ganymede. Without getting her into their line of sight, Kipper didn't think the goons would have enough to go on.

So, her best plan was to keep moving; keep out of sight. That in mind, she dropped low on her haunches and peered around the blue barrels. The white bulldog, Luce, was a distance off, talking to some dock workers. They must have been too absorbed in their grunt work to notice the gray and white streak of fur duck 'n' weaving her way across the floor, because they were scratching their heads and shrugging. The bloodhound was hunched over, inspecting the edge of the growing puddle of Ganymede.

"Where's this water coming from?" he called out to the dock workers. A few of them turned away from their crates and dollies to join in the inspection.

"One of the barrels must be leaking," Kipper heard one of them say.

"Leaking my nose," the bloodhound answered. "Find the 'leak,' find the missing cat. Get on it."

The dock workers, Luce, and the bloodhound fanned out. They were completely unfazed by stepping into the sloshy Ganymede puddle. Kipper could barely stand the feeling of it squishing between her toes. But, she would have to put it out of her mind a little longer.

By now the puddle was big enough (and still expanding) that several configurations of barrels *could* have been the source. The goons and dockworkers were all to one side of her—back toward the docked elevator. So, Kipper went the other way, keeping the blue barrels always between them.

Stepping slowly and surely, to stop the water from splashing around her paws, Kipper made her way to one of the steel arches edging the docking pad. There she found a spiral stairwell. Next to it was a sign bearing a colorful map of the station.

As she read the map, Kipper reflexively tried to shake the moisture off her paws. She lifted one back paw, and then the other, shifting her weight between them. It didn't work. But, when she flexed her claws, she could feel the water squeezing out between her tightened paw pads. Wringing all the water out would take more time than she had. She would have to ignore the feeling of Ganymede between her toes.

The space station map was composed of a number of concentric rings. That way, by spinning, the space station could simulate gravity with centripetal force. The outermost edge of the station—where Kipper wanted to be—was in blue. The cargo bay—where she currently stood—was in black, several rings inward. Which translated to being a few levels above it. So, in two flicks of the tip of her tail, she was bounding along the steps of the spiral staircase. Headed down.

At first, the sound of her footfalls and breathing resounded in her ears. She was sure the bloodhound or Luce would track her to the staircase, drawn by the horrible racket she was making. But it was all in her pointy ears. No barks of "Stop, cat!" came from above. No rough paws grabbed her from behind. She made it three flights down, past a business level, and through a medical section, all the way to the bottom of the stairs. The outer ring. The hub of life on Deep Sky Anchor.

She took a deep breath, flattening her ears in anticipation, and stepped around the last spiral of stairs.

There they were. *Otters.* Otters in suits, like the two on the ferry to the elevator; otters in street clothes—baggy britches and sloppy tunics like the puppy bands of the last decade had made popular; otters of all kinds, living *their* lives, wandering around *their* space station.

It was thrilling. A little like getting a glimpse of what Cat Havana might be like. Except with otters. She wished Petra were here to see it.

It was a little eerie though. All the inhabitants having brushy brown fur, short legs, crazy-long spines, and startlingly self-similar, rounded faces—how did otters tell each other apart? At least, with dogs, they were all different heights and colors. And some of them had beards, like Chip, or elephantine skin like the bloodhound. Kipper shrugged. The otters probably thought all cats look alike. If so, all the better for her, because she still needed to be covering her trail.

To that end, Kipper stepped away from the mouth of the spiral staircase and into the crowd. She was congratulating herself on becoming a part of the *rivers in the sky* when the crowd of otters parted in front of her. And suddenly her breath caught in her throat. Her ears dropped flat against her skull, and her fur even fluffed out a bit. Those rivers... She thought they were a metaphor...

They weren't a metaphor. The crowd of otters thinned and thickened, blocking her view and then allowing glimpses between them. Always behind them, there it was. Blue and rippling, burbling toward her... The river in the sky was a real river, running through the middle of the broad corridor that was the outer ring of Deep Sky Anchor.

Kipper stepped carefully between the otters in the crowd, edging nervously toward the river. When she got to its bank—a deep step in the metal flooring—she turned her head, looking first down- and then upriver. Yes, the artificial river descended as far as she could see into the distance. It must run all the way around the station. A river with no end. Or beginning. Like a snake swallowing its own tail, this river ran.

And the life on the station ran in and out of it. As naturally as... ducks in a pond. Or, otters in a river.

There were cafes with tables right at the edge, chairs knee-deep in the water. Some otters dove right in and swam along like fishes. The middle of the river, clearly deeper than the edges, was like the foot traffic freeway. And, off in the distance, Kipper could see water slides, tributaries joining the central river from either side of the broad, long room all this life was bustling in.

Yes, now that she looked closer, Kipper realized that many of the otters' pelts were wet. And their clothes too. Well, at least her wet toes weren't about to look out of place. Still, her species—and her strangely dyed fur—was sorely out of place. She needed to find something to do about that.

The species... well, that she was stuck with. But, ten minutes of wandering along the bank of the artificial river brought her within sight of a solution to the other problem. A fur tattoo shop. Right across the river from her. It was a dingy lookin' hole in the wall, and the otter running it was completely covered in tattoo dye, but he would have the materials to make her look like one breed of cat again. If she could just get across the river...

Sure, it would be normal and otterly to jump right in, swim across, pat down her wet clothing on the other side. But... Kipper wasn't otterly. She was feline. And, well, honestly, cats don't like to get wet. That one's not a myth.

A few minutes of dithering at the edge of the river, dipping her toes, and generally trying to steel her nerves brought Kipper to an important conclusion. There *had* to be a bridge. So, she continued upriver, enjoying the sights, looking for a dry way across. She wasn't having any luck, but Kipper didn't mind. Her eyes weren't on the river anyway. They were on the sky: huge windows arched above the entire strip. She could see the other rings of the station in their metal enormity through those windows. She could also see the stars.

Kipper's eyes were still focused on the stars, and her mind was in a place all its own, when a troop of otter pups—school age younglings barely up to Kipper's knees—came galloping by. The majority of them went around her, but it only took a few clumsy pups to throw Kipper off balance. She teetered valiantly, every catly instinct trying to keep her from getting wet. Nonetheless, she landed in the drink. Her automatic reflexes immediately kicked in, and Kipper became a blur of white and gray fur, flailing, hissing, and spitting uselessly. It took a concerted effort on her part to control those panic reflexes and pull herself back out.

Of course, she pulled herself out on the wrong side. The side she'd started on. Ears completely flattened, water dripping from their tips, Kipper let out a mournful meouwl. She squinched her eyes shut and crawled back in. She was already soaked to the bone, she might as well save herself another fruitless search for a bridge. Clearly, otters didn't believe in them.

The water rushed past her, pushing her downstream as she struggled against it, toward the farther shore. She crawled out, miserable and scrawny. *A wet cat.* Her fur and clothes were plastered to her from the water, and her purple duffel was dripping like an over-saturated sponge. She felt half-drowned. But, the otters just kept walking by. Bouncing, actually. Their short legs and long, sinuous spines combined to give them all a bouncy, circus gait. Kipper despised them, and their water.

She sat and gasped a while longer, but eventually she had to get up. She wrung out the folds of her green scramball jersey and baggy trousers. She shook her head and could feel the fur fluff up, all spiky with wetness. She must look a fright. Her tail was swishing, and she hadn't even noticed.

Oh well. A fur-dresser would want to wet her fur before dying it anyway. She slunk back along the side of the river, until she once again reached the tattoo shop. Cheap snapshots were taped all over the windows, showing what kind of work the shop could do. Otters were twisted around in the pictures to better display their new fur art. The photographer was clearly an amateur. Faces were fuzzy and out of focus—fuzzier than they should be just from fur.

Most of the otters proudly modeling their dye- tattooed arms or punk stripes in the pictures were trying to look like tough guys. Kipper had trouble seeing an otter who would have to return to a fur-dresser to have his tattoos re-dyed every few weeks as a tough guy. Down on Earth, it was street walker alley cats who hung out at the fur-dresser's. And, when it came down to it, a tattoo shop is just a fur-dresser with attitude.

Kipper shrugged, swung back the door, and walked in.

There were three funny swivel chairs; one was leaned way back so that the otter occupying it could drape himself over it on his stomach. A skinny little river otter was shaving a stripe down the occupant's back. *Very* punk.

Kipper hoped they would be up to repairing her stripes. She didn't want to walk out of here covered in shaved patches alternated with purple spikes.

"Well, hello, Missy Feline," said a grizzled sea otter as he came out from the back. A bizarrely pink curtain cordoned off the back of the shop. It was a very small shop, but the mirrored walls made it feel less crowded. Kipper presumed the mirrors were there so that the clients could watch what was being done to them. She would have to watch them very carefully if she was going to trust this old grizzly bear of an otter anywhere near her fur. "I'm Maurice," he said. "Call me Maury." And the otter stuck his dye-stained paw toward her.

Kipper narrowed her eyes, looking closely at his paw for a moment, and then a sense of peace and acceptance came over her.

She stuck out her paw and shook his vigorously. "I'm Kipper, and I'm usually a gray tabby, but..." Her words broke off as her eyes strayed to the mangled image of her in the surrounding mirrors. She looked like an picture from a kitten's coloring book: only partly filled in, barely constrained by the lines. "Can you fix it? Make my fur look natural again?"

Maury stepped in and put his paws on her. He lifted her arm, brushed his blunt claws along the seam between natural gray and white-bleached fur on her shoulder. He ruffled the fur, one way and then the other. "Cat fur is very thin," he said.

"You've never worked on a cat?" Kipper asked, filled even further with apprehension.

"Not in a long time," he said. He grinned big, seeing her nervousness. "Don't worry. Thinner is easier. Whaddaya want? Back to tabby? Something more exotic?"

Kipper's answer was on the tip of her tongue when she clamped her pointed teeth back together, holding the answer back. She *wanted* her fur back to normal again. The gray stripes she'd seen in the mirror every day of her life, all the way back to when she was peering into that clouded old mirror in the cattery. But...

She'd told Chip she was normally a tabby, hadn't she? She wasn't sure. She couldn't take the risk.

"What kind of cats do you see the most of around here?" she asked.

"I don't..."

"I know," Kipper cut him off. "You don't see many cats. But, when you do, what kinds?"

"I was gonna say, I don't know what the different kinds are called." Maury stretched his bewhiskered mouth again into that wide grin. Between the big, black nose in the center of his face and the rounded grin at the bottom of it—Maury looked the perfect clown. Kipper didn't know how sea otters ever took each other seriously. "Now, I *could* describe them to you."

Kipper dipped her ears submissively: an apology and encouragement for Maury to continue. He didn't continue, and she realized he must not understand feline body language. She'd always taken it for granted that dogs understood—but, they lived around cats all the time. "Go on," she said.

"Up here, it's mostly white cats with dark faces, and flat faced cats —they come in all kinds of colors. We see a lot of those. Well, for cats. Like you said, we don't see *too* many cats up here."

Siamese and Persian, Kipper translated to herself. Persian didn't do her any good; no amount of fur tattooing would give her a Persian's snub nose. And, Kipper shuddered, she didn't relish the idea of becoming one of the bottle-job Siamese she'd always loathed.

"Not liking those options?" Maury asked. "Hey now," he slapped his paws against his thighs suddenly. "I saw a whole troupe of this other kind a couple weeks ago. They had more of your bone-structure than the cats with flat faces..."

"Persians," Kipper provided.

"Right. But, they didn't have that black and white coloring like the..."

"Siamese."

"Yeah. These were built like them but with little gray spots all over. Whole rows of them. I could do your coat up like one of them—doctor those stripes into spots. Easy."

Kipper narrowed her eyes trying to match up the physical description Maury gave her with any of the images of cats in her head. "Egyptian Maus?"

Maury shrugged.

"They all had the gray spots?"

"Oh yeah, any otter who wasn't an expert on fur coloring," Maury dusted himself off proudly, "would have a really hard time telling them apart. If that's what you're going for?"

Kipper weighed her options briefly, but, in the end, she had to admit that fooling otters and dogs was a whole lot more important for the moment than not looking like a fool in front of the... what? ...three, maybe four cats she would run into up here. *Space:* no-cat's land. "Yeah," she said. "That's what I'm going for."

"A cat of mystery," offered the other tattooist, the skinny otter, winking at Kipper via the mirror.

Kipper turned around to face him and saw his client chuckling. He was still lying on his stomach, a white sheet draped over his bottom half. The skinny otter was no longer shaving stripes on him though. Now he was dying the remaining fur purple. And adding spikes. Kipper didn't think he was someone to be doing much judging.

The chuckler hoisted himself up on one elbow and eyed Kipper. His laughing brown eyes were met with a cold green gaze, narrowing in challenge. He chose not to speak, but he kept chuckling.

"Here," Maury said, "let's go in back and work out the details." With one glance from Maury, the purple porcupine lay back on his stomach and the skinny otter bustled back to work, teasing that thick otter pelt into jagged looking spines.

Behind the pink curtain, Maury had a little desk with a computer unit, almost buried by stacks and teetering piles of dusty old books and glossy fashion magazines. He leaned over the chair pushed up to the computer desk, instead of sitting down on it. "What were those spotted cats called again?" he asked.

"Egyptian Mau," Kipper answered, consciously restraining her impulse to drag a paw pad through the layer of dust on a book with a cover that read *Piratical Fur Art*.

After punching a few buttons on the computer's keypad, Maury swiveled the monitor around. The screen hosted several shots of handsome Egyptian Maus. "Is that what you're hoping for?"

Kipper nodded.

Maury turned the screen back and peered closely at it for a while. Another rash of typing, and he said, "It'll take a few hours. Where you still have stripes, I can work with those, but I'll have to lighten the fur around and between them. Your stripes are kind of a gray on gray, but these cats lighten out almost to white behind the spots." He spun the screen around, and pointed to the silvery dappling along a particularly beautiful Egyptian Mau's back. "See, there?"

Kipper nodded.

"The hard part will be restructuring your face and paws. That's what'll really cost you."

Kipper gulped and nodded again. In her nervousness about the impending figure, the price tag on her new disguise, she lost control of her paw: the dust on *Piratical Fur Art* now read "Kipper."

"See, you've completely obliterated the markings on your face," Maury continued, "I'll need to create those delicate little stripe patterns from scratch." He looked at her, then he looked at her paw, doodling in the dust and smiled that ridiculous clown grin.

Kipper pulled her paw away, as if the book had caught fire. She stuffed both white-bleached paws behind her back, and started wringing the green mesh of her jersey to keep them busy. When Maury finally quoted her the price, her eyes widened in disbelief.

"Is that too much for you?" he asked.

"No..." she stumbled. "I mean... That's just fine." Given the price of the elevator ride up to otter space, Kipper figured the price would be much higher. Either Maury was a shockingly philanthropic fur-stylist, or the cost of living in otter space was going to be much more affordable than she'd expected.

It didn't hurt that she still had her life's savings—courtesy of the free ride up the elevator, provided by Chip. "Thank you, Chip," she muttered to herself, as she pulled the neatly folded but slightly damp envelope out of her pocket. She only had to hand over one bill for Maury to throw her a big grin.

"Now, wrap this around yourself, little kitty," Maury shoved a folded white sheet toward her, "and I'll be out front with the brushes and dyes when you're stripped down to nothing but white cotton and," he eyed her home-made dye job, "strangely dyed fur."

Chapter 9

Kipper folded her tunic, trousers, and scramball jersey into her little purple duffle and stowed it beside Maury's desk. She wrapped the white sheet around her, under her arms, and pushed the pink curtain out of her way. Maury was arranging the tools of his trade on the work table beside the closest reclining chair. When he noticed her, he patted on the chair's Naugahyde seat, inviting her to take her place there.

The Naugahyde felt static-y under her bare fur as she seated herself. Before she could really get settled, Maury kicked one of the levers, and the chair thudded back into a full recline.

"Get comfortable, Missy Feline, you've got a long ride ahead of you." And Maury got to work.

Like at a doctor's office, the white sheet spread over her was really a formality—more a mental barrier to make her feel comfortable than a practical physical one. Still, she wasn't at all uncomfortable. The feel of Maury parting her fur and brushing it with the cool dye was relatively pleasant. A light tickle that moved along her ribs, following the pattern of her stripes.

Despite the occasional uprising by the Church of the First Race, nakedness just wasn't that big of a taboo. It would never take much more than an unusually hot summer to get even the most dogmatic, puritanical dog—who prayed daily for the First Race to return—to strip down to only the skimpiest pair of shorts.

The furry peoples of the world could never be as deeply attached to clothing as all the history books suggested humans had once been. It's just not practical to get too attached to a coat of cotton when you're already wearing a coat of the finest fur.

"Want a drink?" Maury asked, putting his tools-of-the-trade down and heading to the back. He returned with an unidentifiable bottle and held it out to her after taking a swig himself. "These stripes are going to take awhile," he said, "So, I thought some refreshments were in order."

"What is it?" Kipper asked.

"Symilk."

Kipper looked confused. The other fur-dresser, who seemed to be just about finished with the purple otter, came over to take a swig from the bottle and saw her look of confusion. "Symilk," he said. "Synthetic milk." The skinny fur-dresser handed the bottle back to Maury, and he held it out to Kipper again. She shrugged and took it.

"They probably don't have symilk down below," the purple otter said, rising from his reclined chair. "They've got cow-dogs rasslin' up the real thing."

Kipper was still examining the symilk, swishing it around in the bottle. She figured it couldn't hurt to drink it, so she took a quick sip. The gulp of symilk went down fast. The flavor was right... She had to give it that. But, it was thin. It didn't creamily coat her tongue and sooth it's way down her throat like real milk would. Like milk should. No, this was no replacement for the "real thing."

"Besides," the purple fellow was saying, holding his paw out for Kipper to pass the bottle. She handed it off without any regrets. "Besides, there isn't any space up here for dairy farms." He gulped at the symilk showing much more relish for the beverage than Kipper felt it deserved. He wiped a purpled paw across his whiskers before continuing. "Even if otters did like fraternizing with cows as much as dogs do. We're just not as much in to pretending to be humans."

"Well, that's the real reason," the skinny otter added, beckoning for the bottle to make it's way to him. "Only dogs raise cows, and you can't get a decent price on anything with a dog monopoly on it." He took a swig and handed the bottle on to Maury. "If we could," he shrugged, "we'd buy it. Ship it up the elevator with all the other Earth goods. I mean, you can get a decent price on planet side fish."

"Sure," the purple one said. "Any dog, cat, or otter enjoys fishing. It takes one of those weird Collies or Corgis, a real cow dog—*herd* dog—to want to spend any time around cows."

It was strange listening to otters talk politics. Kipper felt a burning ambivalence about them and their talk. Part of her was fascinated and wanted to fall into their world. *Become* one of the otters if she could. Another part of her was as indifferent to their petty problem importing milk as they must be to the struggles of her people. Why did the otters have so much power and control of their own lives? And cats so little?

And, yet, as the otters continued to talk and pass the symilk around, Kipper found herself feeling a strange sensation. She felt like *defending* dogs. It was odd. But... She liked having real, fresh milk, instead of this thin, synthesized stuff. And, like the otters, she didn't want to raise cows. So... Actually... She kind of admired all the shepherd dogs out there who did that for her. They were good, hard-working dogs. Like Trudith.

And, although Trudith tended to order too many rich, red meats for the comfort of Kipper's stomach, Kipper did like the taste of a juicy, rare steak now and then. This world in the sky, run entirely by otters, probably didn't have those.

A world run entirely by cats wouldn't either.

Kipper drifted further into her own thoughts as the otters deepened their debate of socio-economics and living on a space station. Eventually, Maury capped the nearly empty bottle of symilk and returned it to the refrigerator that must be hiding in the back with his desk. While he was gone, the purple otter turned to Kipper and asked, "So, what do you think of it?"

"Er... what?" Kipper asked, quickly trying to pull any of the otters' recent comments out of her ears, where they were still echoing around—not quite making it all the way to her brain. "Well, the dog monopoly on..." she started, hoping to find her way as she went. But, it was too late. She had no idea what she was being asked to comment on.

Now this otter would look at her like she was so used to dogs looking at her: with the smug look that said, "you can't expect a cat to understand anything." It was bad enough getting that look from hare-brained dogs like Trudith. She didn't think she could stand it from an otter covered in alternating stripes of bare skin and spiked purple fur.

But before the twitch at the end of Kipper's tail could work its way up to a smart remark on her tongue, the otter laughed and said, "*Symilk*. How do you like it?"

"Oh..." Kipper said. She looked at him, searching his brown eyes under spiked brows for mockery or malice. She couldn't find any. He raised the purple brows, expecting an answer. "It's thin," she said. "Thinner than real milk."

He smiled. "You get used to it."

"Is it any good for cooking with?" Kipper asked.

"I don't know. My tugboat's got a galley."

The purple guy seemed to think that explained everything. Kipper looked at the otter quizzically. "Your tugboat?"

"Yeah, the *Jolly Barracuda*."

The skinny tattooist, who was putting away all the scissors and razors he'd used fancying up the purple otter, snorted. "Trugger works on a cargo ship, Miss Feline. He thinks he's a pirate. The whole ship's worth of them think they're pirates."

Trugger bristled. Of course, he was already quite bristly from the purple spikes, but he still looked bothered by the skinny otter's tone. "I don't think I'm a pirate," he said.

"No?" the skinny one asked. "Then how come you come here wanting to be made all tough looking like that?"

"I'd watch your mouth," Trugger advised. "You wouldn't want to convince me *not* to come here any more, would you?"

The skinny otter chuckled and put his paws up in surrender. "If you stopped coming, we'd lose our best walking advertisement in the red quarter. Soon as we could turn around, we'd be out of business."

Trugger looked mollified.

"But, we haven't answered the fine lady feline's question. I cook," he said and turned to Kipper. "Symilk works fine in sauces and soups. And most baking. But it gives you a little trouble in custards. It doesn't thicken quite right."

"Because it's thinner," Kipper said, but her mind was further back in the conversation.

The thin otter shrugged his narrow shoulders. "Something about the chemical structure. Of the proteins."

Maury returned from the back and got back to work on Kipper's stripes while the skinny otter returned to tidying his work area. Trugger was gingerly pulling on a jacket over his spikes when Kipper called out to him, asking: "Heading back to the red quarter?" And, saying those words, she realized why they were familiar.

Trugger started answering Kipper's innocent question with an involved explanation of scheduling export shipments from the asteroid belt, but Kipper wasn't really listening.

She reached to dig through her pockets for confirmation of her new thought, but her trousers were still folded neatly on Maury's desk. The white sheet wrapped around her wouldn't have the crumpled, torn half of a ticket receipt hidden anywhere in it, and she couldn't get up and fetch her trousers without interrupting Maury's work. But, Kipper didn't really need to look at the receipt. No, she was sure. *Red 1/4* was one of the cryptic scrawlings on that treasure map to the adventure she was on.

As Trugger continued explaining about the inter-planetary art scene (apparently the exports from the asteroids were mostly *objet d'art*), Maury moved from her back and sides to working on her paws.

As Maury doctored her body stripes, Kipper got away with twisting around, occasionally, trying to glimpse how it was going. Maury admonished her, however, to quit fidgeting now. He'd be inventing stripes free-hand on her paws, so he needed them completely still.

She complied easily enough. Her entire focus had moved from watching Maury's work to steering Trugger's topic of conversation. He was clearly a naturally chatty otter, but she wasn't interested in the fine line the captain of the *Jolly Barracuda* had to walk between outright piracy and essential black market smuggling. She needed to find out as much as she could about the *red quarter*.

Fortunately, Trugger seemed perfectly content to stay and talk while Maury painted the stripes on her paws. By the time Maury pronounced the left paw done, Kipper had heard all about the in-fighting between different merchants who docked in the red quarter, where the name came from (the red docking lights around the air-hatches), the best restaurants near the red quarter (apparently, a pair of immigrant squirrels ran Trugger's favorite), and, most importantly, a rough idea of how to get there from Maury's. By the time, Maury pronounced the right paw done, she'd been given a complete rundown of the menu at the squirrels' restaurant, along with recommendations for which dishes were best at which times of day.

Even though Kipper was done with Trugger now, having learned what she needed from him—and more—he showed no interest in leaving. To her slight annoyance, he kept chattering away while Maury did the most terrifying part of his job: recreating the stripes on her face.

Kipper didn't like the dyes and brushes so close to her eyes. She fought the reflexes to squeeze her already shut eyes more tightly shut. That would interfere with the dying, and she didn't want crooked stripes.

Trapped in the dark world behind her eyes, Kipper's mind kept coming back to what Maury had said about her bone structure. Sure, it was the opinion of an otter, but even so. She was deeply flattered by the idea that he thought she had a regal bone structure like Siamese and Egyptian Maus and all those breeds of cat that are brought up in rich, purebred homes—houses strewn with silk pillows. She knew it wasn't really like that, but it was how she pictured their lives anyway.

It only took one orphan at her cattery lucky enough to have perfect Siamese points being adopted by a couple in a button down suit and a blue dress (it matched the adoptive mother's Siamese eyes) to stamp that image very deep in Kipper's brain. *If only she looked like that*, she'd thought, *maybe she'd have been adopted too.*

Kipper began to feel a little bit of hope about the final outcome of this entire dubious venture. Maybe this otter tattooist was a greater artist than the low-class, down-trodden cat fur dressers on Earth. Maybe she really would look like a purebred cat.

It seemed like forever, but finally, Maury was done.

"Take a look," Maury said, giving her chair a spin so that Kipper faced the closest mirror by the time her eyes were open. "So?" Maury asked, holding up a hand mirror so Kipper could see herself from all sides. "What do you think?"

"It's a complete transformation," Trugger answered, admiration in his voice.

Maury smiled, accepting the compliment, but he was still watching Kipper. She would be the true judge of his work.

"She looks all regal and fancy, like those cats you see in vid-dramas."

"Yes, thank you, but what does the Miss Feline think herself?"

Honestly, Kipper didn't know what to think. She kept peering at the mirror, trying to find herself in this foreign face of another cat. A purebred Egyptian Mau. And, then, her perspective would flip and all she could see was a botched and blotty Kipper—no sign of Egyptian Mau anywhere in the exaggerated, white and black, Halloween-ghost mask that Maury had made of her. No true Egyptian Mau had coloring this pronounced.

And, yet... Maybe she just had unusually distinct markings. It wasn't completely unbelievable.

By now, Maury was looking a little nervous. Kipper suspected he was confident of the quality of his work, but it's never fun to have an unhappy client.

Trugger, on the other paw, was grinning broadly. "Look at that, she's so taken with her new coat that she can't even find her tongue to answer you. Cat's got her own tongue!" He laughed and slapped his thigh. He was still chuckling as he headed for the door. "Well, *Kipper*," he said, just before leaving, "maybe I'll catch you in the red quarter..." The door swung shut behind him.

An uncomfortable moment ensued. The skinny otter had come up behind Maury, and they were both waiting. They were probably trying to come up with ways to supplicate the wrath of an unhappy cat. Ways to make her just happy enough with the coat to walk out the front door without demanding her money back.

But, uncertain as she was of her new appearance, Kipper couldn't think of a single way to change it for the better. She needed this disguise, and this disguise looked as good as it was going to get. It looked, in fact, better than she had expected.

Kipper finally pulled herself together enough to dip her ears and throw Maury an appreciative smile. "Thank you," she said.

Chapter 10

As the bill was already settled, Kipper had herself dressed and back out on the main drag in no time. She caught herself looking at the otters around her, trying to catch their reaction to her in their eyes. She wove between them, staying as far away from the artificial river as she could manage. She didn't want to get tripped or pushed into the water again. The otters, by and large, gave her a respectful amount of space. Perhaps they understood what she was doing. She imagined herself walking in the paw steps of all the other cats who had come to this station and who carefully edged their way away from the water.

Of course, her behavior didn't go completely unnoticed. The otters looked at her as she edged around them. They looked at her, and they held their gaze longer than she expected. They looked at her, and they smiled. Kipper began to fear it was a condescending smile. Perhaps because they knew she was afraid of the water. Or, perhaps, because they were quietly laughing at her new coloring.

On Earth, a dog wouldn't look at a cat on the street for longer than it had to. Longer than it took the dog's eyes to pass the cat over and move on to something safer to look at. And a dog wouldn't smile at a strange cat for no reason.

So, clearly, there must be something comical about her that made them look and smile. Except... The further she walked and the more closely she watched the otters, the less that felt like the case. These smiles didn't feel like they singled her out of the crowd. These smiles were bouncing all over the crowd. These smiles were being shared between otter and otter.

Maybe otters just smile at strangers more than dogs.

Maybe, otters just smile more than dogs. Or cats, for that matter.

Kipper continued to follow the curve of the river, upstream like Trugger had described. As she understood it, the red quarter was very near the giant cargo bay where bloodhound and bulldog had chased her across puddles from Ganymede. However, she could get there from the other side, without passing that minefield, if she followed the river far enough—basically, if she followed the river all the way around. A handy aspect of living on a torus.

As she understood it, the space elevator unloaded into a cargo bay on the docking ring. All the above board, official, completely honest shipping business took place right there, by the elevator. The red quarter was on the opposite side of the docking ring, as far away from the space elevator cargo bay as the cut-throat pirates and "honest" black-marketeers (like Trugger's hard-working captain) could manage to be, while still actually docking their ships on the docking ring.

Of course, since Kipper was walking around the outermost ring of Deep Sky Anchor—necessarily the largest ring—she would have to walk a long way to get there. But, she didn't intend to keep it that way.

After the equivalent of a couple of New LA city blocks, she made her way to the edge of the wide room housing the river. There was another spiral stair that matched the one she'd come down before. In fact, they were apparently staggered along opposite sides of the river. So, she could have avoided swimming across the river before by climbing up a level, crossing there, and climbing back down a stair case on the opposite side. If only she'd known.

Kipper mounted the stair and spiraled away from the noise and tumult of the river. It was clearly the center of otter life on this station. The other levels she passed while spiraling toward the innermost docking level were deathly quiet in comparison.

Before emerging again on her desired level at the top of the stair, Kipper paused to catch her breath. Center herself. Convince herself that there wouldn't be dogs waiting to arrest her.

She did draw a few stares when she rounded that final spiral and stepped up onto the docking ring floor. That was only to be expected. There aren't many cats in space. But, the otters and dogs she saw were all otherwise occupied; they weren't looking for a runaway, stowaway cat. So, they didn't look at her for long before getting back to their real work: moving crates and boxes, loading and unloading docked ships. Kipper breathed a deep sigh of relief.

She didn't know where she was going, precisely, but Kipper automatically turned away from the end of the cargo ring where she had begun. By coming back to the docking ring, she knew she was re-entering the territory of Chip's hired bloodhound and that white bulldog, Luce. But, now, every step took her further into the red quarter, and farther away from them. So, with every step, she relaxed a little. She dug her paw in her pocket and pulled out the crumpled receipt with her scribbled directions:

"@ SE, ask for Chip—night flight—DSA, red 1/4—Larson w/ the *Manta Ray*"

If Petra was up here, those were the words that would guide her. Her heart raced a little at the thought that so few words might stand between her and her sister now: "Larson w/the *Manta Ray*."

Larson must be Violet's final contact, and, perhaps, the *Manta Ray* was a space ship? If so, would it still be here? Violet had started out several days ahead of Kipper, and she took the shortcut to Ecuador. The road trip through Central America with Trudith had put even more time between them. By now... Well, if the *Manta Ray* was waiting to take Violet somewhere, she could already be there. At Cat Havana. Or wherever else she'd decided to go. Wherever Sahalie had sent her...

Could that really be true? Could Violet and Sahalie have really been working together? The fact that Sahalie's money seemed to be behind the space elevator "night flights" implied it. But... Kipper still found it hard to believe.

None of that mattered though. Kipper was in space now, without enough money to get back down. She had no where else to go, so she might as well go forward. Kipper's ears flattened in consternation and concentration. She needed a way to find out where the *Manta Ray* was or, if it was gone, where it had been heading.

With her ears flat and her eyes focused on the scrawled words "*Manta Ray*," as if she could summon Larson (whoever *he* was) out of words themselves with her gaze, Kipper practically walked into Luce.

She was deep in the red quarter, by now. And most of the otters around looked like Trugger, tattooed and dyed beyond recognition. Okay, most of them weren't as extreme as Trugger, but there was barely an otter who still sported a fully brown coat. Luce should have stuck out like a sore thumb, but Kipper hadn't been looking. And, in her defense, Luce was shorter than the otters. (For Kipper's pride, Kipper hoped Luce had been standing behind one. For her future safety, Kipper wished *she* was standing behind one now. Or several. Big ones. Who liked defending strange cats...)

Fortunately for Kipper, Luce was looking the other way. She was snarling—maybe Luce didn't mean to snarl, but her bulldog grimace turned her face into a snarl anyway—at a bunch of otters. Unfortunately, she was asking them if they'd seen any cats around, and right as Kipper was going to breathe a sigh of relief that Luce hadn't seen her, one of the lanky, young-lookin' otters pointed right at her. Luce swung her head around for a quick look, but Kipper's disguise must have worked. Luce turned right back to the otters and snarled, "Not a spotted one, a white one. A white one wearing a..." Luce trailed off, and Kipper realized she'd made a horrible mistake.

After all that trouble to dye her fur, she was still wearing the same green jersey.

She started to back away, but Luce was already coming toward her. Eyes locked on her. Trying to make a break for it would just confirm what Luce already suspected, and then she'd be on the run again with a blown disguise. So, Kipper planted her paws firmly on the ground where she stood and waited for the bulldog to approach. Acting as if she didn't care. Maybe, by some miracle, Luce could be convinced that this wasn't the cat she was looking for.

After a broad look up and down, Luce snorted through her foreshortened nose. "Where'd you get that green jersey?" she asked.

"I bought it at a thrift shop on the outer ring."

Luce snorted again. Kipper hoped that all of Maury's toxic dyes combined with Luce's useless-looking, foreshortened nose would be enough to protect her from being recognized by smell. Given that Luce hadn't laid paws on her yet, Kipper guessed it was.

Thank goodness she'd run into Luce instead of her bloodhound partner.

The moments stretched on, and Kipper tried to imagine the thoughts going on behind Luce's wrinkled forehead. *Was there another cat running around wearing a green jersey? Was there a whole team of cats wearing green jerseys? Was this spotted cat trying to cover up for her white-furred, green-jersey-wearing teammate?* Kipper had to concentrate to keep from snickering. She didn't really believe Luce's thought processes would be so laughable, but she could hope.

Since Luce hadn't actually tried to detain her, Kipper decided to try moving on her way. It didn't work.

"Wait," Luce said. "I need to ask you a few more questions." She reached a stubby arm out and wrapped a dull-clawed paw around Kipper's upper arm. "Let's go find my partner."

"I haven't done anything," Kipper said, digging her claws into the metal flooring. The *scree* of the metal under her sharpened claw tips was unpleasant, but Luce kept dragging her along regardless.

Kipper was still trying to decide between fight, flight, and continuing to protest her innocence when Luce flipped out a vidcom with her free paw. The bloodhound popped up on the little color screen. "Luce?" he said. His voice came out tinny in the tiny speakers. "What've you got?"

Kipper tried to ease away from the vidcom, but Luce's grip was too firm. She thought about leaning out of the vidcom's video range, but that seemed too awkward and suspicious. She'd just have to hope the bloodhound wasn't any better at recognizing a fur-job by sight than Luce.

"I found a spotted cat, dressed like the one we're chasing. Smells similar too, but I'm not sure."

"I dunno, Luce," the bloodhound said. "We're looking for a white cat."

"Coulda dyed her fur."

"And not changed her clothes? Not even a cat is that dumb."

Kipper fumed. But kept it quiet. The only thing worse than being *that dumb* would be being *more dumb*. She wouldn't compound her stupidity by denying it. In one stroke, revealing herself and proving Luce—*a dog*—right. And, in this case, a dog was right. It happened. Sometimes.

"Look," the bloodhound continued, seeing that Luce was less than convinced. "I called down to Chip a few minutes ago, and he said this cat will be heading for the *Manta Ray*. So, why don't you drag the spotted cat along, and I'll meet you there?"

"Sure," Luce agreed and pocketed the vidcom again. "Let's go," she told Kipper before beginning to drag her along. Perhaps Kipper should have struggled, argued that she had somewhere else to be. But, she'd forgotten her role of innocent Egyptian Mau entirely when she heard that the *Manta Ray* was still docked. The bloodhound was right—again—that was exactly where she was headed. And it made her very nervous that he knew that. Though, it didn't change her plans; the Manta Ray was the one place she could hope to find some answers.

Of course, she would rather not arrive effectively handcuffed to Luce. Nor at the same time as a bloodhound who would have a better than even chance of recognizing her scent. He had already proved himself pretty smart for a dog.

No, it would be much better if Kipper could give Luce the slip and then follow her there.

To that end, Kipper needed a distraction. She looked around, but nothing seemed imminent. None of these otters were going to unknowingly cooperate with her. So, she'd just have to do the best with what she had: a purple duffel bag and a believable outrage at how Luce was treating her.

First step. As an otter passed by, almost brushing Kipper's shoulder, she slung her purple duffel down and kicked it. Then, she stumbled as if she'd tripped, tangling her hind paws in the otter's. The otter crashed down, rolling into a tumble of paws and fur with her.

A little dazed, even though she'd known the fall was coming, Kipper pushed herself off the cold metal floor. She was winded, and the otter looked at least as phased as her. "Are you all right?" the otter asked. Kipper could tell from the voice and clothes that it was a woman otter. Though, despite years of watching otter television, she still had trouble telling the slight differences in physique between male and female otters apart on sight.

"Yeah, I'm fine..." Kipper started to say. It was true, and it was polite. And she wanted to be polite to this hapless otter who wouldn't know why Kipper was about to flip out at her. But she needed a scene. So, she fought her civilized impulses and readied herself to hurl insults and accusations at the otter for tripping her and kicking her bag.

She didn't need to.

Before Kipper could say anything, Luce jumped in and started doing it for her. Everything Kipper could have thought of to say— reasonable or not—Luce did say. Kipper and the otter stared wide eyed at her, as the string of vituperative invectives hurled from Luce's jowly mouth grew and grew. Any unenlightened bystander would have thought the otter woman was personally responsible for stealing and hiding the First Race away from Luce and all her devout, bereaved dog brethren. Not merely tripping over a cat.

"I'm sorry..." the otter woman mumbled, sounding horribly shamed. But, then, another otter, who couldn't help listening to Luce's voluminous tirade stepped in with his part: "Don't *you* feel sorry about upsetting *this* dog! I've never heard anyone be more rude, and I didn't see you do anything wrong!" He reached to help her up, kindly putting a paw out to Kipper too.

"*Water breathers*," Luce growled. By then, there were even more otters gathered around to take offense at Luce's racial slur. "Interfering with my cat. All sticking together!"

"Your cat?!" Kipper cried out. Her outrage was automatic, but she couldn't have chosen a more perfect response or set a more perfect timbre to her voice. The otters immediately rallied around her.

The otter who'd helped her and the woman otter up emerged as the un-elected spokesman: "I don't know what you're used to down *there*," the contempt in his voice shook his whiskers as he spoke, "but you don't own cats or anyone up *here*."

"She's my captive!" Deep behind the sags of skin and red rims, Luce's eyes were shifting madly among the growing circle of otters. Better than that, since she and Kipper were already deep in the red quarter, it was a growing circle of otter renegades, black marketeers, and—to use the tattooist's word—*pirates.*

Kipper grinned, watching and slowly backing away as the scene she'd started spiraled completely out of control. Apparently, the red quarter otters had a long backlog of issues with Earth law (possibly law in general), dog enforcers (probably law enforcers in general), and Luce, specifically. Kipper had given them the excuse they needed to vent a little.

As much as she felt Luce deserved a taste of her own medicine, Kipper was glad to see that the otter throng didn't descend past a few shoves and raised voices. "Get back to your quarter!" one otter shouted; another followed with, "Go back down to *Earth.*" But, by and large, as the otters had their say, they felt satisfied enough to leave the mob. Become individuals again. So, one by one, the otters left Luce standing in the middle of the hall, seething, eyes darting— probably looking for Kipper. But, the distraction had provided more than enough time and cover for Kipper to reacquire her duffel and squeeze behind a nearby docking fixture.

She crouched close to the floor, hoping Luce would continue scanning the crowd at head height, and peered between the metal flanges of the gear-like protuberance providing her dog-blind. Not much more than her eyes and whiskers could be showing, and even those were in the shadows. Moreover, Kipper knew that Luce's sense of smell wasn't what a dog's should be. Still, her heart leapt when Luce wrinkled her nose while looking nearly at her.

Then, Luce stomped her paw, grumbled, and gave up. Her expression must have meant disgust and resignation—not the hint of a feline scent. Kipper allowed Luce a solid head start before slipping out from her hiding hole to trail her. Better to lose Luce than have Luce *un*lose her.

Chapter 11

Trailing Luce would have been easier for Kipper if bulldogs weren't so much shorter than otters. Between Luce's short, boxy shape and Kipper's own limited height, Kipper felt constantly on the edge of losing Luce in the crowd of irritatingly tall otters. Of course, on the flipside, the large (albeit generally lanky) stature of all the space station natives kept Kipper from having to duck and weave too much to stay safely obscured from Luce's view. "*Too much*" being a relative term.

The only thing that kept Kipper going when Luce disappeared around a blind corner or when an otter gave her a strange look for dodging suddenly behind a stack of crates was her immense need to find the *Manta Ray*. She'd come so far to find her sister. She'd traveled through more than a pawful of countries and off the very planet. After traveling so far, with only a ridiculous crumpled up receipt as her guide, she had too much invested to turn back. If she couldn't find her sister, she could at least take her place. She would find Cat Havana for Petra or look like an idiot trying. That's what Petra would do.

Even so, the entire process did make Kipper feel like an idiot. Skulking about, jumping out of sight at the slightest provocation— either she was a very bad spy, or spies had a stupid job.

Luce came to a sudden halt, and Kipper nearly walked from behind a blue coverall-ed otter right into her. She made a quick recovery, jumping straight backward and dodging behind a parked self-loader. All of her fur fluffed out from the fright, and the coverall-ed otter laughed at her.

Yes, an idiot. That's how pretending to be a spy made her feel. *A complete idiot.* And that was before the worst part:

Kipper crouched behind the self-loader wondering what was taking Luce so long. The white bulldog was just *standing* there. Looking at something. Kipper crept around to the front of the self-loader, making sure to keep an otter between her and Luce, trying to get a better look. She bobbed about ridiculously for a minute or so, dealing what felt like a mortal blow to her cat pride. When she finally got a clear view without revealing herself, Kipper's whiskers literally drooped.

Luce was taking so long because she was staring at a large electronic signboard. On the board was posted a twinkling LED manifesto of currently docked ships.

Luce didn't know where the *Manta Ray* was any better than Kipper—she was reading its location off of a list. Kipper could have asked *any* otter she passed to help her find the *Manta Ray*. They all would have pointed her to that list.

A whimper caught in Kipper's throat. It was the dying spasm of her cat pride. This was the final clinching proof that she really was stupid. Or at least, a *terrible* spy.

Still, when Luce continued on her way, Kipper followed her. She no longer needed Luce to find the quarry of her final clue, but what did she have to lose? She had no pride left, and she hoped...

She didn't know what she hoped.

She'd simply invested too much in trailing this dog, pretending to be a spy, to give it up now and admit to herself it had been pointless.

So she continued doggedly on, sticking with Luce even as the albatross of a bulldog took several wrong turns. Finally, the berth of the *Manta Ray*, with an impatiently waiting bloodhound pacing out front, came into sight.

Despite the two dogs who were actively searching for her with who knew what ungodly plans for her in their minds, Kipper couldn't help the relief that filled her at the sight of her quarry. There was the ship that had taken Violet away from all this dog nonsense. Or maybe, it was the ship Violet was still on? Either way, Kipper believed there were allies on that ship; she was almost sure enough to walk right past Luce and the bloodhound, counting on the otters inside to see her, recognize Violet's kin—another cat who was tired of being dog-trodden, working for dogs, living under a government run by dogs, and being stuck on a world filled with dogs.

And yet... It was Sahalie who sent Trudith after her and turned Chip against her...

"I was just in talking to Larson," the bloodhound said.

Even if Larson and all the other otters inside the *Manta Ray* were her allies, Kipper had followed Luce here at great cost. (A cat's pride is worth a lot to a cat.) It couldn't hurt to play out this game of spy. *Play it safe.* She was to the easy part now... So, Kipper sidled up against the station wall, shielded from sight by a jutting support beam, and listened.

"He hasn't seen any *stray* cats," the bloodhound continued, still clearly audible. Kipper didn't like the way he stressed the word "stray." "Where's the cat you found?"

"She got away."

Luce's shamefaced sounding answer made Kipper's ears perk up with glee. She risked peaking around the support beam. The bloodhound looked unimpressed.

"There was a problem with some of the otters," Luce defended herself. "Almost a riot... I lost her in the crowd."

The bloodhound treated Luce to the kind of patronizing look that Kipper enjoyed from dogs like him all the time.

"Probably wasn't the right cat anyway..." Luce mumbled.

"That's what I said."

"Just an awful coincidence, you know, both of them wearing green jerseys like that." The coincidence clearly still bothered her. Ironically, despite all of Luce's incompetence, her first instinct was right. Kipper was tempted to make a splashy entrance and throw Luce into even greater confusion. She suspected that there wasn't much more to learn from eavesdropping on these dog goons. Then, suddenly, the entire situation changed: a decidedly non-stray cat appeared, tentatively, from the inside of the *Manta Ray's* entry hatch. *It was Violet. She was still here.*

She might not have kept a picture of herself on her desk at Luna

Tech, but Kipper was willing to play the odds on this one. Just as there weren't two cats running around Deep Sky Anchor wearing green jerseys, there weren't two clear blue eyed Siamese women hanging around the *Manta Ray*. This was Violet.

In a deep, throaty voice Violet said: "The otters said you were out here." Her regal bearing, the tone of her voice, the very shape of her eyes—everything about Violet shamed Kipper in her faux-Mau fur. "Is there a problem?"

This cat had fled dogs all the way into space, and Kipper had brought those same dogs right to her. But, then, Kipper noticed a strange thing. Luce and the bloodhound weren't looking Violet in the eyes. Luce was shuffling her feet, and the bloodhound nearly stuttered as he said, "There's a stray cat."

"There are lots of stray cats," Violet said. "Why do we care about this particular one?" It was strangely empowering to hear a cat use the same patronizing tone with dogs that Kipper was used to hearing *from* dogs.

"She's been masquerading as one of you. She presented herself to Chip just like all the others."

"And Chip let her on the elevator?" Violet's voice rose dangerously at the end of her question. The dogs looked terrified. Kipper was confused.

"We'll find her," the bloodhound offered.

Violet's ears flickered flat, but she had them tall again before the moment passed. "It doesn't matter. If Chip can't tell the difference between a paying customer and a mere stowaway, he'll be replaced. Or the otters will notice all his underhanded dealings. Either way, the crew of the *Manta Ray* is much clearer-headed, so this *stray* won't get any farther. Do what you want about her."

And, like that, Kipper found herself alone in space.

There was nothing for her on the *Manta Ray*. No refuge from the dog goons. No friendly, fleeing-feline waiting to explain the mystery that had pulled her here.

And wherever Petra had gotten to... She wasn't here, and she wouldn't be getting here. Chip wasn't likely to help another cat *masquerading* as one of Violet and Sahalie's crowd bum a ride, and Kipper knew Petra couldn't afford a ticket.

Unless, Kipper thought with a touch of hope, *Petra had beaten her to the elevator...* But, no, Chip and Violet had made such a big deal about Kipper sneaking through. Petra couldn't have come before her. Kipper's paws felt like phantoms on the beam she was hiding behind. Her entire body felt like something foreign she didn't belong inside. She began backing away, not knowing what to do or where to go. What would Luce and the bloodhound do with her if they caught her? Did the otter authorities care about stowaways from the elevator? How could she get home?

What would Petra do?

She had to make some sort of decision soon. Luce and the bloodhound had finished talking to Violet, and, although they hadn't seen her yet, they were heading her way. Kipper turned—wherever she went, it should be away from them—but, before she made it a full step, she ran into the broad brown (and purple) chest of an otter.

"Hey! Missy!" the otter said.

Kipper looked up into the grinning face of Trugger.

"You decided to come and visit? Take me up on my offer of a tour of the grand ol' *Jolly Barracuda?*"

Vague memories of feigning interest in Trugger's ship and Trugger pressing her to let him show her around resurfaced in Kipper's mind. All she'd really wanted were directions to the red quarter.

"Um..." she said, looking for an escape, but all she saw was Luce and a disgruntled bloodhound bearing down on her. "Um, yes. Yes, I'd love a tour." Anything was better than standing, aimless and lost, directly in the path of those goons.

"Great!" Trugger said and swept his zebra spiked arm behind her, guiding her away from the *Manta Ray* and back toward the *Jolly Barracuda.* His gesture also had the inadvertent effect of shielding her with his bulk from the dogs' sight. Kipper walked safely in Trugger's shadow all the way along the curve of the red quarter until they reached the *Jolly Barracuda's* berth. Then, she was cheerily invited off of the crowded, public strip—where a short bulldog could be hiding behind any tall otter—and into the private safe-haven of the legendary Captain Cod and crew.

"Welcome aboard," Trugger said with a flourish. Then he began her tour. He walked her up and down the halls of his craft, chattering away as he was wont to do. This time, Kipper didn't mind.

The *Jolly Barracuda* was Kipper's first real space ship, and, even though she'd spent the afternoon on a space station, she couldn't help a quiet rumbling from swelling in her throat as she stepped through the open hatchways and airlock onto the deck of a vehicle that traveled between planets. The simple thrill of it made her purr. Suddenly, she felt back on track. She didn't know what Petra would have done about Violet, but she knew Petra would be proud to see her here.

The ship itself wasn't anything like Kipper expected. It was cramped with winding little hallways, and the walls were covered in a cheesy, fake-wood paneling. There were iron grates periodically in the floor and ceiling, and everything felt musty and damp. A sterile, toxic smell like the chlorine at a dog's public swimming pool pervaded the air. She choked on it when she tried to breathe too deeply, so she kept to short, shallow breaths.

Strangest of all were the paintings. They were hanging everywhere. Large oil canvases in gilt-edged frames. Encased in clear plexiglass. As if they were hanging in a museum—except, museums don't entomb the paintings like that, only objects. Coins and daggers, little things that could be walked off with.

The scratched plexiglass distorted her view, but Kipper wasn't enough of an art expert to care about the brush strokes anyway. And these didn't look like ancient masterpieces.

They mostly sported fantastic representations of old human-style sailboats, except the boats sailed among the stars. Swashbuckling on the high... vacuum? Or perhaps ether. Space seemed to swirl with a haze of purple dust in most of the paintings, and the ships were manned with heroic, gallant looking otters. Except, the characters weren't all otters. There were dogs and cats, too. Even squirrels and birds and reptiles. And humans. Fanciful.

Kipper had to admit a certain charm in the world the paintings conjured. All species living together, living high on the seas of the sky. She wondered about the mind behind their selection, but she didn't have to wonder long.

"Captain Cod at your service," a burly otter said, sticking his webbed paw under Kipper's nose, presumably for her to shake it. She took the risk, as it seemed polite, despite fearing his paw would be wet. It wasn't. Apparently, otter fur simply has a natural, oily sheen that makes it look always wet. And probably water proofs it, but Kipper didn't know for sure about that. "Where's your visitor from, Trugger?"

"Where are most cats from?" Kipper asked, feeling a little peevish.

"Good point! What brings you up from the ol' solid rock?"

Trugger chuckled and said, "I found her at Maury's."

Kipper could see the captain looking her over, examining the fur job Maury had done—or maybe looking for it. Given what Trugger went to Maury's for, Captain Cod probably found her fur disconcertingly natural. Which seemed fair. His gaze was disconcerting her. And, since she felt disconcerted, she covered with sass: "I'm a spy," she said. "I've been following someone."

Trugger and Captain Cod were both clearly delighted. "What a lark in a larch!" the captain exclaimed.

Trugger looked more contemplative: "That's why you had Maury do the Egyptian meow-y job?"

Kipper hadn't expected the word "spy" to earn her so much credit so quickly. "Actually," she said, "that was just to shake some dogs who were chasing me. The cat I've been following has never seen me. She didn't even know she was being followed."

"Cats following cats," Captain Cod mused. "*Intrigue.* I always knew that was what you felines were all about. Well, we might be able to use a spy on board."

Kipper couldn't see how. But she was stranded up here in space, and she wasn't about to point out the numerous flaws with the idea of a cat spy working among a population composed ninety-five percent of otters if the captain couldn't work them out for himself. These were the only friends she had so far, and, if Trudith had taught her anything, it was that she shouldn't underestimate the value of friendship. Even the friendship of seemingly bumbling, incompetent dogs—or eccentric otters. Which reminded her... "Captain, are you the one who picked all these paintings?"

"Aren't they a lark?" the captain said, not quite answering her. She dipped her ears in a gesture any cat, and even most dogs would recognize, but the captain just grinned at her. Apparently, these otters were going to take some training to read a cat properly. Kipper clarified with a rolling gesture of her paw. This time he got it. "Right, yes, I picked them. They're from an artist commune in the asteroid belt. We ship their paintings, show them around to art dealers, and sell them for a commission. But, these were too good to pass on right away." Captain Cod looked proudly at the nearest painting—a sunscape, featuring a dashing otter swinging on a solar flare as if it were a vine and he were a monkey in a jungle.

"Yes," Kipper said, "I can see that. Far too good to pass on."

"Well, right away, anyway," Captain Cod amended, ponderously. "Do you think..." he began, looking at Trugger, but he trailed off and chewed his whiskers instead of finishing.

"They seemed pretty adamant," Trugger replied, regardless of the incompleteness of the captain's sentence.

"Indeed. Yes. Well, it's not as if we'd be ready to part with the paintings yet." The captain looked doubtfully at the nearby painting, and, as he did, his face brightened right up. It was as if the gaudy orange and yellow oil sunbeams had reached right out of the painting to fall on his face like real sunlight and cheer him.

"No," he said, "I can't imagine passing them on. It just wouldn't do. Look at they way this painting livens up the corridor!"

Kipper had to admit that the dank tiled floor and plastic paneled walls were better off for the distraction the painting provided.

"Anyway, I seem to have interrupted your tour," the captain said. He looked at Trugger. "I assume you were going to show the feline lady around." He looked back at Kipper, raising his otterly brows. "It's a splendid ship. A real singing lark. A skylark even."

"I'm sure," Kipper said.

"Well, I'll leave you two to that. But, do bring her by the bridge before letting her go, Trugger. I'll want to know what you think of my skylark," he told Kipper. "She's never had a cat on her. Not since I've been captain anyway..." Captain Cod kept talking as he walked away. Eventually he got far enough along the corridor that Kipper could only conclude he was talking to the ship. Not her and Trugger.

"He's a great captain," Trugger said. "Really stands by his principles."

Before Kipper could ask exactly what Captain Cod's principles were, Trugger resumed his role as tour guide, telling her about the history of their ship. Apparently, it hadn't originally been meant for cargo hauling, which was its primary function now. "Although, our cargo hold is empty at the moment... See there's been a bit of a misunderstanding," Trugger looked as if he would explain further but then thought better of it. Instead he returned to the story of how Captain Cod won the *Jolly Barracuda* in a poker game, securing her future as a cargo ship—a noble and honorable vocation for a ship, to hear Trugger tell it—rather than an experimental military vessel gathering dust due to the lack of any war for her to fight in. Kipper couldn't tell which use Trugger deplored more for his beloved ship— war vessel or dust bunny.

The tour took Kipper from stem to stern. Trugger didn't explain much about the ship's workings. He was more interested in telling stories about the exploits of Captain Cod and the brave, daring crew he worked among. Kipper couldn't tell if Trugger was a new initiate to the *Jolly Barracuda*, still glamoured by having been invited to join, or if he was really that naturally exuberantly enthusiastic.

Or, maybe, she was a tired cat, and any otter giving her a tour of a spaceship would have worn her out. Come to think of it, Kipper hadn't slept since her last nap in the car while Trudith drove. That felt like days ago.

"This way's the galley," Trugger said. "You've got to meet our chef."

"The one you mentioned at Maury's?" Kipper asked, making an effort to regain her focus. Instead, everything went fuzzy and echo-y. The physical drain of hauling boxes for Chip, the stress of running and hiding from Chip's goons, and the sheer number of hours since she'd slept all added up.

"Whoa, Miss Feline," Trugger said, putting a paw out to steady her. "You look like you're..." Before he could finish the sentence, Kipper fell into a swoon. The fake wood wall and one of Trugger's arms protected her from landing on the floor, but she still found herself leaning against Trugger as he insisted on walking her to the barracks and settling her in his bunk.

"You can meet Emily later," he said. "In fact, I'll have her whip something up for you to eat. Do you like chowder?"

Kipper tried to say that she'd never had it, but her own body felt a million miles away. She couldn't get to herself fast enough to make her tongue work. Instead, she heard Trugger tell her, "It doesn't matter. You just rest for now, and I'll be back to check on you later."

Chapter 12

Kipper couldn't remember falling asleep, but she could tell she had just woken up. She was stretched out on a thin but cushy mattress, a bottom bunk in a room full of bunks. There were otters occupying some of the other beds, but none of them had noticed her yet. Well, she was sure they knew she was there. But none of them had noticed she was awake. She didn't want them to. She wasn't ready to deal with a room full of strange otters yet. She had too much to deal with inside of herself.

Strange otters. She repeated those words again in her mind.

That's what surrounded her now. Everywhere. Not just in this room of bunk beds on a bizarrely plastic-wood paneled spaceship. But everywhere. Strange otters. And their strange ways. In their strange places.

And she had no way home. Nor any assurance she would be safe there, if she could get there. The money in her tunic pocket wasn't enough to get her from Earth to space; it wouldn't be enough to get her from space back to Earth. So, like it or not, even though she no longer had any clue what she was doing here, Kipper was stuck in space.

The smell came first, then the stirring of the otters around her in the other bunks. "What's that?" one of them asked. "Has Emily put chowder on?"

Kipper opened her eyes a little and curled herself inward, making herself smaller. She could see Trugger at the end of the room, a steaming bowl in his paws. The creamy, fishy smell was wafting in that steam. Enticing. And it was coming her way.

The other otters were clearing out, probably heading towards the galley and a tureen of chowder. Kipper didn't have to work that hard. Trugger brought the steaming bowl right to her and sat down beside her on the bunk, proffering the bowl. Kipper thanked him and took it. Resting on her haunches, bowl cradled in her paws, she put her nose right to the surface of the creamy-thick, white soup. She smelled fish, shellfish, and real milk. "This isn't made from *symilk*," she said.

Trugger shrugged. "You'd have to ask Emily. Try it."

The chowder was heavenly. Milk and seafood. The two most perfect foods, making a most perfect combination. This simple bowl of soup was a much better meal than the steak dinners Trudith had treated her to. This wouldn't sit like lead in her stomach. It filled her, warmed her, and left her feeling satisfied.

"You look like you feel better," Trugger said.

"Yes." Kipper put aside the empty bowl. She refrained, with difficulty, from licking it out. "Sorry about the fainting. I hadn't realized how long it had been since I'd slept. Or eaten..."

"No need to worry. We Jolly Barracudas take care of any foundlings that fall into our nest."

The tone of Trugger's comment made Kipper think he didn't know that barracudas were a vicious kind of tropical fish. The image of a nest full of barracudas, high in the branches of a tree, waiting for hapless little birdies to happen on them did make her smile. But she was sure it wasn't the image Trugger meant to conjure.

"So, why *did* you fall into our nest?"

Kipper flicked her tail tip, ticking off time with its pendular motion. Every answer she could give Trugger led to another question. The path of answers would take her so far back, it made her head spin.

"It's a secret," Trugger ventured. "You're a spy. I should have known that."

"No," Kipper said. "It just doesn't matter anymore. I failed at what I was doing. And now I don't even know what I'm doing here. In space."

"Space is a great place."

"For otters. Have you seen how few cats are around?"

Trugger rubbed his forepaws together and then slicked his whiskers. "I can't deny that. It doesn't mean you're not welcome. In fact, you're very welcome here. The *Jolly Barracuda* tends to run a little underhanded..."

"Are you offering me a job?"

"That wouldn't be my place," Trugger said. "Captain Cod makes all those decisions. He's smart about... Well, everything. But, if you asked him, I'll bet he could find a place for you here." Perhaps Trugger could see that Kipper looked doubtful, because he added, "We're a fine crew." He squared his shoulders, lightly touching one paw to a pin on the lapel of his vest. It was a gold pin, shaped like one of the sailing ships from Captain Cod's adored fantastical paintings. Then, he grinned. "It'd be fun to have a cat in the crew. We'd be the only smugglers, er, marketeers with a cat on board, let alone as one of the crew."

"Well, that's not quite true," Kipper said. "That cat I was following..."

"Yes?" Trugger prompted.

"Well, that's where I lost her. She's onboard the *Manta Ray*."

"They're scoundrels," Trugger said. Then, after a thoughtful pause, "I wonder why they've taken a cat on board?"

Kipper's ears flattened in consternation.

She didn't think Trugger understood the meaning of flattened ears on a cat, but he must have understood something in her look, because he added, "The *Manta Ray* blokes aren't the friendliest otters. Not very outgoing. They barely associate with us other marketeers. So, I can't imagine they'd bring an outsider on board for anything other than business."

"Maybe she hired them to take her somewhere," Kipper said. In her ears, she heard the echoing words *Cat Havana*, but she didn't say them. Trugger wouldn't have understood what they meant to her. Or at all.

"That could be," he said. "The *Manta*s do run courier sometimes. I haven't heard of them taking passengers, but they keep most of their business pretty hush-hush. So, it's entirely possible."

Kipper was almost reluctant to ask the question, because she hoped too much from the answer: "Do you know where she could be going?"

"On the *Manta Ray*?"

Kipper nodded, her ears flickering. She was fighting to keep them proud and tall. Even if Trugger didn't know what their flagging height meant, the straightness of her ears meant something to *her*. It was like fighting to keep your smile, because you know it's all that's protecting you from crying. Except, Kipper wouldn't cry, because she knew better than to expect the answer she wanted from Trugger.

"Like I said, they keep their business pretty hush-hush."

Kipper sighed under her whiskers. Even if Trugger had known where Violet was going on the *Manta Ray*, Kipper wasn't sure any more it would be an answer she wanted to hear. Cats like Sahalie— and Violet too, she supposed now that she'd seen her—weren't the type to be fleeing dog purgatory for cat heaven. They were too conniving, sneaky, and—dare she even think it?—*catty* to need an escape from dogs. Instead, they just twisted dogs around a carefully extended pinky claw.

The thought of it made Kipper retract her claws, making her paws harmless and velvety. She didn't want to be like that. She hoped her relationship with Trudith couldn't be seen that way. Kipper sighed. Everyone she knew and cared about was so far away...

"Of course," Trugger suggested, still following the lines of their conversation, "it might not be impossible to find out. Not for a crack team of otters—the first to employ their own feline spy." Trugger's eyes got all dreamy for a moment, and then he snapped back to reality. "I'm getting ahead of myself," he said. "Let's go talk to the captain." So, Trugger bounced up from the cot they'd been sitting on and offered Kipper a paw. She didn't need the help getting up, but she took his paw to be courteous. They left the emptied chowder bowl abandoned on the bed and headed toward the front of the ship to find Captain Cod.

Trugger's earlier guided tour of the *Jolly Barracuda* had started Kipper in the back of the ship, with the cargo hold. From there, they'd worked their way forward until Kipper fainted. Now, they finished their forward march, coming all the way to the foremost room on the ship. The bridge.

Trugger explained that the bridge and living quarters were all gathered near the front of the ship, with cargo areas in the back, for some reason involving atmospheric pressure, acceleration simulating gravity, and fluid dynamics. But, like with his stories about how Captain Cod won the *Jolly Barracuda* in a poker game—despite it being fixed against him—Kipper wasn't listening all that closely. She would regret that later.

For now, she was excited and a little overwhelmed to take her first steps into the control room and bridge of a spaceship. It wasn't as if the ship transformed from the tacky plexiglass and fake wood into gleaming panels and glowing buttons with those steps. The fake wood was as present here as anywhere. However, she could feel that she was at the ship's hub. Monitors lined all the walls, and every other surface was covered in switches, levers, and keypads. She could picture the room busy, bustling with otters while the *Jolly Barracuda* was in flight, performing some complicated docking maneuver or course adjustment.

Now, of course, the bridge was mostly quiet. Captain Cod was consulting with another river otter by a flickering console. The rest of the crew must have been down in the galley, eating Emily's chowder. Or otherwise away. Perhaps roaming the station. Kipper wondered how long their trips between ports lasted. Did the otters get cabin fever and long for their "rivers in the sky?" She hadn't seen any swimming pools on board, but, from what she knew of otters, Kipper found it hard to imagine that the *Barracuda* crew would be willing to long forgo their native urge to swim.

"Well, if it isn't our visiting kitty-cat," said Captain Cod, catching Kipper and Trugger's reflections in the screen he was watching. He turned to face them. "That was quite a long tour, wasn't it? I take it that you liked our fine ship."

Kipper nodded and searched for a truth she could say that would sound complimentary: "Yes, it looks quite... sea-worthy."

Captain Cod brightened with a broad otter grin. "*Space*: the great sea of the sky." He spread his paws expansively. "Now, I asked you to come see me after your tour."

Kipper dipped her ears in acknowledgement. Then, she clarified with an accompanying nod.

"Right," the captain said. "Why was that?" There was a baffled pause since neither Kipper nor Trugger knew quite why the captain had wanted to see her. "Oh, I remember! The cat *spy*," he said. "Well, well, well, I can't miss an opportunity like that. I've heard a rumor about chowder in the galley. Why don't we go there to talk? I may even have a proposition for you."

So, Captain Cod and Kipper left Trugger and the otter at the console to watch the bridge. The two of them headed for the galley, and, along the way, Captain Cod insisted on stopping to discuss almost every painting hanging on the corridor walls. So, by the time they reached the galley, most of the throng from the barracks had already cleared out. The remaining few passed Kipper and the captain as they entered with salutary hails and politely disguised curiosity. The former for the captain; the latter for Kipper.

The only person left in the galley was Emily, the cook. At least, Kipper assumed it was Emily. But she wasn't what Kipper would have expected. At all.

The galley featured two rows of long, rectangular tables bolted to the floor. They were the same fake wood design as most of the walls. Then, in the back, behind a plexiglass shield was the kitchen, flooded to the ceiling with water. Emily was busy inside arranging the stores in the cupboards, sharpening her chopping knives, and updating her shopping list on a computer panel. At least, those were the tasks Kipper could figure out from looking at her. All Kipper knew for sure was that each of Emily's sinewy, suction-cupped arms was busily doing *something*.

From Kipper's limited knowledge, she guessed that Emily was a *Giant Pacific* octopus. Kipper only knew two breeds of octopus— Giant Pacific and blue-ringed—between those two, Giant Pacific was a pretty safe bet.

Kipper had heard rumors that octopus society had advanced beyond anything cats and dogs were doing, but she hadn't expected to see one here. In space. In Kipper's mind, outer space was otter society. Despite the squirrels running a diner in the red quarter... At any rate, she thought octopuses were still keeping to the oceans. Apparently not Emily.

"Kipper?" the captain inquired, for Kipper had stopped still at the sight of Emily. She was still transfixed by the curling, undulating motion of her tentacles. "Kipper?"

"That's Emily?" Kipper asked.

"Oh! Yes, our chef. I didn't realize Trugger hadn't introduced you yet."

Kipper's ears flattened at the horrific image of herself ever entering that flooded kitchen to meet Emily: treading water, holding her breath, *drowning*. No, swimming was not for cats. Especially not for Kipper.

"Is there a hatchway?" Kipper asked, trying to figure out how the food made it between the kitchen and the rest of the galley. "Oh, yes, I see it..." She peered harder at the transparent, plexiglass wall dividing the room; it had a double hatch on the top of a bar counter, with a device that looked a little like a blender on the side. Probably a suction pump for emptying the hatch of water before opening it on this side. The safe, dry side. "Does Emily ever come out of there?"

"What?" Captain Cod exclaimed, "you don't think we keep her locked in the kitchen all the time? Do you?"

"Well..." Kipper didn't want to admit that she had been wondering.

"She sleeps in the barracks with the rest of the crew. Except when we're docked, of course. She has a cubbyhole in the back of the kitchen, kind of the octopus version of a cot, I guess, for while we're docked."

While he spoke, Captain Cod began making the strangest series of gestures with his paws. Quick, expansive motions. Kipper was utterly baffled, and he laughed at her expression.

"Sign language," the captain said. "I was just introducing you to Emily." He pointed at the flooded kitchen, and Kipper looked back to see that Emily had put all her knives and canned goods aside. She was sitting—standing?—on the counter, her golden eyes staring through the plexiglass and across the room at Kipper. "Go ahead, wave to her. You don't know any SSS, do you?"

Kipper shook her head dumbly.

"No, I guess not," the captain said. "That's *Standard Swimmer's Signing*—SSS. Well, here's your first lesson: waving means the same.

So, go ahead."

Kipper trepidatiously raised a paw and flexed her claws outward, stretching her paw into a wave. Emily immediately reciprocated, lazily swaying a mottled tentacle. She looked like a window-washer, trying to wipe the plexiglass window between them clean. Well, a very strange window-washer. A very strange *anything*.

While Kipper stood dumbstruck, the captain proceeded across the galley to the counter dividing the dining area from the flooded kitchen. A giant, squat, metal pot sat on the near side of the counter, in front of the plexiglass, a little to the side of the hatchway it must have come through to leave the kitchen. Captain Cod grabbed a bowl from a stack of them at the end of the counter and ladled the creamy white glop—less steaming than when Kipper had eaten it—from the pot and into his bowl.

"Now, this is the good stuff!" Captain Cod said raising his bowl. He moved to the nearest dining table and seated himself on the bench with the sloshing full bowl before him. "Care to join me?"

"I already had some," Kipper said, but she joined him at the table anyway.

"Lucky cat," he said. "Emily only makes us chowder when we're docked. And only then when we beg her."

"Why only when you're docked? Are the supplies perishable?"

"Swimming ostriches, no! Well..." the captain looked ponderous, "I suppose if you really did chowder up right, you would have to get some fresh shrimps and salmon... But, no, we get all that stuff canned."

"Swimming ostriches?" Kipper asked.

"It's an expression. See, it would just be too messy when we're flying with the oxo-agua atmosphere."

"Can ostriches swim?" Kipper asked, not realizing she was missing an important point. Trugger had mentioned *oxo-agua* earlier while she was tuning out his lecture on practical spaceship physics, so she was old hat at ignoring that technical term by now.

"Actually," Captain Cod said, "they can swim. They're awfully funny, ungainly looking when they do it though. It's a real lark in a larch to watch." So, Kipper missed her second opportunity to be warned about the situation she was about to get herself into. She was a cat about to be thrown into a vat of water. All too literally.

"Anyway..." the captain continued, sobering up from his reflections on swimming land birds and settling down to business. "I've got this problem. See, all the paintings? For a while now, we've been transporting and dealing them for a colony of artists in the asteroids."

"I think you mentioned that," Kipper said.

"Well, there's been a misunderstanding. And they don't want to work with us anymore." The captain stared levelly at Kipper. She got the idea that she was supposed to be offering a solution to his problem, but she couldn't imagine what kind of solution he expected. Or, more to the point, why he expected it from her. "So..." The captain stirred his soup. "So... You're a spy."

Kipper still wasn't sure what he wanted.

"Spies know things. They know people. They have connections."

"You want me to hook you up with another art supplier?"

"Do you know one?" The captain looked eager.

Kipper twisted her ears about in confusion. "You do realize I just got here? Yesterday, I was down on Earth." The reality wasn't hitting him. "And, a week ago I was a temp in an office. The only person I've ever spied on is this one cat—Violet. And, I think I'm done with even that now."

The captain's whiskers drooped, but he quickly covered his disappointment with a spoonful of chowder. "Well, it was a long shot," he said between mouthfuls. He set down the spoon again. "So, why are you done spying on this Violet? You finished the job?"

"More like failed at it. I trailed her to the *Manta Ray*. The trail ended there."

"What were you trailing her for?"

Kipper locked her eyes on the table; she couldn't answer Captain Cod's question while looking at him. "I hoped she was fleeing Earth to get to a Cat Havana. Some sort of utopia where cats run their own government and their own lives. And live together without dogs controlling them." She felt silly saying it. But, Captain Cod was such a silly otter that somehow she managed to anyway.

"That's lovely," he said. They were both quiet for a while. Then, he asked, "Where was she actually going?"

"I don't know," Kipper answered. "Like I said, I lost her at the *Manta Ray.*"

"Then, you don't really know that she *isn't* going to a hidden utopia run by cats. I wonder what kind of art a place like that would deal in... A bunch of felines hopped up high on utopia could probably conjure some crazy-swimmy art."

Kipper lowered one ear questioningly. Captain Cod's leap from *her* imaginary Cat Havana to *his* role as sole art dealer for all the hypothetical cat artists there—well, it was a bit much for her. "Even if Violet is going to a hidden colony of cats..." she pointed out, "they seem to already have an established relationship with the *Manta Ray.*"

"No one in their right mind would rather work with slimy ol' Larson and his barnacle bogged *Manta Ray* than with the upstanding crew of the fine, sky-sailing *Jolly Barracuda!*"

Kipper had to wonder if Captain Cod was in his right mind, but she knew better than to argue with him when she heard his following plan:

"Look, you want to know where Violet is going, and I'm looking for a new trade route for my cargo ship. You've already done the first thing I'd want from you as ship's spy—er, *information specialist.* (It wouldn't be very spy-like to call you a spy, now would it?)" he added under his breath. "Anyway, you've set me on a lead—all I have to do now is follow it. And that's an excellent beginning to your job. If you'll take it."

"Wait, you're planning to follow the *Manta Ray*, hoping to find a hidden colony of cats, so that you can offer your services to them in place of Captain Larson's?"

"That's the general idea. Want in?"

"Yes," she answered. "Yes." It didn't matter to Kipper that Captain Cod's plan was crazy. He was offering to subsidize the next portion of her trip—a portion she had thought unattainable at any price. Certainly any price payable by the scanty cash folded up in her tunic pocket.

"You'll take the job, then?" The captain looked excited. "You'll be a *Jolly Barracuda?*" He was about to be the first otter to captain a spaceship with a cat on the crew. He nearly jumped out of his seat when Kipper nodded.

"Sweet-singing lark!" he exclaimed. "Well, let's go get you set up. You're okay with staying in the barracks with the rest of the otters? You've seen the barracks? Trugger can show you the ropes..."

Chapter 13

Captain Cod set Kipper up with her own bunk in the barracks and personally pinned one of the golden sailing ship lapel pins on her tunic. It made her feel very official. Officially an honorary otter.

There were also some electronic forms; Trugger helped her fill them out. As far as she could tell, she was registering to pay taxes on the modest salary Captain Cod afforded her. She wondered if there was any way for the dogs down on Earth to claim a portion too. She hoped not.

Once all the work was done, Trugger took her around and personally introduced her to each of her new shipmates. Besides her and Emily, there was only one other woman on the ship. Jenny, a petite, dark-furred river otter offered to show Kipper around the space station, specifically to help her pick up any supplies she needed. Like a few changes of clothes. Trugger decided to tag along.

Jenny helped Kipper scour the local tailor shops and thrift stores for any clothes that would fit a cat. Mostly, the pants were too short and the tops too long. Everything was designed to suit the short limbs and long torso of an otter. Nonetheless, Jenny had a good eye and was able to help Kipper pick out a few things.

Afterward, Trugger showed the ladies to his favorite squirrel restaurant, the one run by immigrant squirrels. He chittered in a foreign tongue to the squirrels and ordered clam juice and appetizers all around. Kipper had to admit the nut mash was pretty good, and clam juice, she decided, was definitely worth drinking. A lot.

Fortunately, it sounded like the *Jolly Barracuda* kept a full stock.

By the third round of clam juices, Jenny excused herself. She had a few station-dwelling friends to visit before the *Jolly Barracuda* put out to deep space. According to public station records, the *Manta Ray's* berth was only reserved for another day. In order to tail her, the *Jolly Barracuda* would also put out tomorrow. And, according to Trugger, it could be weeks or months before they arrived anywhere.

He regaled Kipper with tales of his past trips through deep space over the fourth and fifth rounds of clam juice. Then it was time to go. Kipper felt like she'd barely had time to realize that she was really in space, let alone explore the *Deep Sky Anchor* as much as she wanted.

Nonetheless, Kipper had enjoyed her one afternoon of otter-culture touristing.

The last errand Kipper insisted on running before retiring to the ship for the night was to put in a call to Alistair. He didn't answer, but she wasn't surprised. She left a message: "Ali, it's me. Kipper. I made it to the space elevator. And up to the station. Petra isn't here, and I don't think she's coming. I wish I could get a message to her... I hope she's okay." Kipper clenched her teeth, flattened her ears, and forced herself not to worry about Petra. "Nothing's been going like I expected... I can't afford the ride back down. But, these otters offered me a job. And they might help me find out what that cat, Violet, was up to... I don't know. We're leaving tomorrow, and, well, I just wanted you to know."

Kipper felt so cut off. Everything she'd ever known was a hundred thousand kilometers away. Her closest connection to her brother right now was Trudith, who she'd left behind most of a day ago. "Oh, right," she said. "I sent that dog I was traveling with—Trudith—I sent her back to look out for you. Or for you to look out for her. But you should know that by now... 'Cause, if you're watching this, then she got you out of jail..." Kipper trailed off feeling confused and even more disconnected. "Well, tell her 'hi' from me," she ended lamely. She hoped Alistair was out of jail by now. She wondered what he'd done to get in there.

Then, Kipper stepped back and let Trugger take over. He explained how Alistair could call a message in to the communications hub at Deep Sky Anchor. That way, Kipper could access anything

Alistair had to tell her at the *Jolly Barracuda*'s convenience. And at a semi-reasonable cost. It was much cheaper, apparently, for ships to call in to the communications hub for messages than for the communications hub to actively locate a ship, catch its attention, and then transmit messages to it.

Once the errands were over, Trugger brought Kipper back to the ship, where the evening threatened to stretch on forever. Kipper packed her new belongings away in the drawers under her bunk, and she listened to the otters throw stories about during dinner in the galley. She was exhausted, but, when she settled down to sleep in her bunk, she could barely sleep. She was too nervous about tomorrow. Although, she wasn't half as nervous as she would have been if she'd realized exactly what was coming.

She should have known. It was an otter spacecraft. Every few feet, there was an iron grilled drain in the floor and ceiling. Everything that mattered was made from plastic. The paintings were protected under plastic. And, most importantly, Trugger had even explained it to her.

Nonetheless, Kipper dismissed the first dampness she felt on the floor of the *Jolly Barracuda*. There was so much craziness—everything hectic—with all of the crew rushing about, preparing themselves and the ship for flight. Kipper assumed the water she felt between her toes had simply been tracked in and dripped about by one of the hurried otters who had been recently swimming in the space station's artificial river. She didn't worry about it.

Instead, she darted about the ship, dodging otters, and looking for a good window to perch by during take-off. She'd been trapped inside a dark, cargo bay for her arrival at Deep Sky Anchor. She intended to have a better view of the station as she left it.

Eventually, she picked an oblong window with a bench seat beside it. The seat was upholstered in a plasticky foam and was reasonably comfortable. Most importantly, the window and bench seemed to be mostly out of the way of the busiest parts of the ship. So, Kipper settled down to await take-off. Only then did she realize that the dampness in her toes hadn't dried off.

In fact, the floor around her bench was wet.

At first, it was only a thin film of water. But, as she watched, with rising horror, the thin film grew thicker. Clearly, this was more than a little water tracked about on the floor by a careless, water-loving otter.

She wondered why the otters hadn't noticed and whether she should warn them. Before she had time to decide what to do about it, she found herself sloshing through enough water to splash about when she stood up. There was no way the otters hadn't noticed it. *Why weren't they concerned?*

As the level of the water rose and the level of concern (namely none) displayed by the otters she passed didn't rise, Kipper found herself closer and closer to panicking. She looked at the impassive faces of the otters rushing about. They saw nothing wrong with the now ankle deep water. It must be a normal part of take-off. A horrifying thought.

Kipper tried to remember what Trugger had told her about fluid dynamics yesterday during the tour. It hadn't seemed pressingly important at the time. But, it seemed more and more pressingly important now. Of course, the more she started to panic, the less she could coherently think to remember Trugger's words.

She reached a paw out to the nearest otter. The solid feel of his shoulder under her quavering paw steadied her slightly. "How high is the water going to rise?" she asked. The otter she asked simply laughed and grinned before hurrying on his way. She thought she'd fall without the otter as a prop to lean on, but she couldn't stand the idea of falling into the water. The *rising* water.

She caught herself. And looked for another otter. The next nearest otter was working a maintenance panel on the wall. She thought, maybe, he had overheard her. So, she looked to him, hoping for an answer. But he just winked.

Kipper didn't like that at all. "Where's Trugger?" she asked.

She could have pressed the otter for a straight answer to her original question, but she strongly suspected she wouldn't like the answer. She was halfway sure that she'd put the pieces of this highly distressing puzzle together. On her own. She didn't know what she hoped to find from Trugger. Possibly reassurance. He was the otter she knew best. The closest thing she had to a friend out here in space.

Unfortunately, the otter she asked didn't know where she could find Trugger. So, she headed back to the barracks, her field of vision narrowing into a dark, watery tunnel. *Slosh, slosh*, she went, wading now down the hallways. *Slosh, slosh* is not a way cats should go.

The water was almost to her waist.

Soon, she'd have to swim. It wasn't right. Her breathing was becoming ragged and labored. One step, one dragging, water-impeded step at a time, she made her way to the barracks. But she couldn't lie down on her bunk when she got there. It was already under the rising level of the water.

Complete and utter panic.

"Kipper?"

She heard her name, then she felt the webbed paws on her shoulders.

"Kipper?" Trugger said. "I heard you were wandering the halls, not looking too good."

Kipper's eyes were too unfocused to find Trugger's, but she looked in the general direction of his face. In the barest whisper between her pointy teeth, she said, "How high? How high is the water going to rise?"

She'd already figured out the answer for herself, so she was hardly even listening as Trugger said, "It's not water. It's oxo-agua. A highly oxygenated liquid atmosphere."

Kipper's eyes were dilated, and Trugger could tell his words weren't meaning anything to her. "How high?" she asked again.

"You're going to have to breathe it." He looked at Kipper and realized he was going to have to walk her through this.

"I've got to get off..." Kipper rasped. "Get me back to the station!"

"Just stay calm," Trugger said. "We've already sealed the airlocks and disembarked, but you don't really want to leave anyway."

Kipper sputtered, too frazzled to effectively communicate how very, *very* much she *did want to leave.* The water was up to her chest now, and her lungs felt heavy with panic already. It wasn't quite as high on Trugger, since he was taller. "Look," Trugger said, trying to recapture her attention. "It's just like being weightless." He stopped for moment, thinking. "Well... not just like being weightless, 'cause you'll feel how the up and down of everything becomes more subjective when we hit our travel velocity..." He could see he was losing her.

Trugger took Kipper's paws in his; her claws pierced the soft webbing between his toes, but he just flinched and took it. "We're going to duck under the water. Okay? We'll just duck down and come back up."

With a little hopping and swaying, keeping his paws held tight on hers, Trugger managed to urge Kipper downwards. Their heads submerged, and the oxo-agua pressed around her. Water entirely around her; in her ears, her nose, her eyes... Kipper gasped when they came back up.

"See? Not so bad."

Kipper didn't entirely agree. In fact, she didn't agree at all. But, she nodded. Dumbly. Her focus locked on Trugger. Trying not to panic.

"Now we're going to do it again."

Oxo-agua (which Kipper found indistinguishable from water except for Trugger's word that it wasn't) dripped down all the crevasses of Kipper's face and filled all the cavities. It was a horrible sensation. But, before she could shake it off, Trugger was pulling her down again.

"This time," he said, just before submerging, "open your eyes and look around."

She tried to follow his instructions. It took a great effort of will to fight her natural instincts. She wanted to keep her eyes squeezed tight shut. The oxo-agua didn't sting her eyes like she expected, but the world around her was wavery and blurry. And her lungs were bursting for air. She shot back up and gasped the air, gulping it down, once she was above the surface again. Dispiritedly, she realized the surface was higher now. Just under her chin.

"You're doing great," Trugger said. Considering that it was Trugger's first time guiding a cat into breathing a liquid atmosphere, Kipper thought he was doing great. That belief disappeared with his next words: "This is the last time. We'll go under. Open your mouth. And breathe it. You'll be fine."

Kipper wanted to scream at him that he was crazy, but he moved so fast that he'd already pulled her under. And she couldn't, just couldn't follow his instructions this time. She couldn't even try.

Instead, she opened her eyes to the bleary wateriness of oxo-agua, beseeching him with her look to change the world. Make the water go away. Put her safely back on Earth, surrounded by bully dogs who only insulted or threw things at her. Occasionally tried to beat her to death. But they never, never tried to drown her. That's what he was doing. His firm grip on her utterly restrained her from trying to resurface. She tried, briefly to struggle, but she knew it was only a matter of time before there wasn't a surface to return to. Only a hard, metal ceiling. No, she didn't want to claw and scrabble and gasp at the last, thinning air at the top of the room. She wanted to follow Trugger's instructions. She could see him breathing, easily, calmly in front of her. But he was an otter. They can breathe water, can't they?

The longer she looked at Trugger, his purple stripes fluffed by the oxo-agua he floated in, the less he looked like an otter. The more he began to look like a bizarre, tropical, space-fish. Everything was blurring. It wasn't long after she wondered whether space-fishes could breathe vacuum that the world blanked out.

All was fuzzy silence when she awoke. And the strangest sensation of thickness. She stirred and felt herself rise above the surface she was resting on. Was she falling? She opened her eyes and grabbed out for something to hold. She opened her mouth to scream, but the sound didn't come out right. Muffled. Strangely small and high pitched. Almost inaudible. "Where am I?" she asked, but she couldn't hear that any better. A sob caught in her throat, but the air in her throat was already thick...

It wasn't air.

Oxo-agua.

Another sob.

Before the third sob, Trugger was beside her, webbed paws steadying her. He made a series of gestures. They looked familiar... like the gestures Captain Cod used to communicate with Emily. But Kipper didn't understand them. She could feel the panic rising again, but Trugger squeezed her shoulders, took her paw, and led her up from the bunk. This was the second time he'd had to bring a blacked-out Kipper to the barracks. She felt ashamed and tried to make up for it by docilely, gamely following his lead. It was hard. Cats aren't built to swim like otters. *She* didn't have webbed paws. Or practice.

With a little trial and error, however, she managed to wobble her way through the oxo-agua after Trugger. They didn't go far. He'd led her to a computer console; Kipper suspected it was the nearest one.

They were in a small room just down the corridor from the barracks. Trugger didn't have to seat himself at the computer. He more...*floated* at it. That bothered Kipper.

Still floating, Trugger put his paws to the computer keys, and in a flash the monitor read, "You don't know any sign language, do you?"

Kipper shook her head.

More typing, and the monitor read, "I didn't think of that."

Awkwardly, Kipper tried to maneuver herself toward the computer. She kept grasping at it, her paws sliding away empty through the oxo-agua, until finally one paw hit solid matter. She grabbed the edge of the desk and pulled. That was much easier, and she was soon able to type: "Captain Cod knew."

Trugger frowned. Rolled his eyes. And then shrugged. He took over the keyboard again. "You'll just have to learn."

Kipper flattened her ears, feeling very aware of the thickness of the oxo-agua inside them. Trugger was cruising through the files on the *Jolly Barracuda* computer system at a mile a minute. He grinned when he found what he wanted and pointed at the screen. Kipper tilted her head looking at it.

"Standard Swimmer's Sign: A Tutorial."

She sighed, and the oxo-agua streamed thickly through her throat and lungs. This was the beginning, she realized, of what life among otter pirates would be like. Swimming. Studying and "speaking" a foreign language. Swimming. More swimming. Everything foreign.

Even her most constant companion, who she had expected to be Trugger, turned out to instead be the most foreign person on the ship.

Most of the otters, including Trugger, were kept busy by their onboard jobs, keeping the ship smoothly running. But, Kipper wasn't experienced with spaceship maintenance or operations, so she had a great deal of free time. And Swimmer's Sign came faster to Kipper than expected. Especially since she hadn't expected to be studying it almost full time.

Most of the gestures were reasonably intuitive, and Kipper didn't have much else to do during their stealthy flight in pursuit of the *Manta Ray*. So, over time, she came to spend most of her days in the kitchen, practicing her signing skills on Emily. While the otters seemed foreign in their manner, build, and personality to Kipper, they were blood brothers to her in comparison to Emily.

Practicing with one of the otters might have been easier, since Swimmer's Sign was essentially two languages: one used by otters and an entirely separate one used by octopi. With all those limbs... and no hands... Well, you just couldn't expect an octopus to make the same "hand" signals as a creature with paws. In fact, Emily's signals were really much more subtle and complicated.

However, Kipper didn't mind the added challenge of discourse with Emily. The octopus chef of the *Jolly Barracuda* had a far too interesting history for Kipper to begrudge the work it took her to ascertain it. And, besides, there was nothing else to do. Watching the stars hang steadily in the windows lost its charm after the first few days. Well, not entirely. But, it couldn't fill all her hours.

Kipper did continue to spend her mornings gazing through the unchanging windows. She took her breakfasts to where she could keep an eye on the large, palely colored dot that she'd been told was the *Manta Ray*. Boris, the pilot who sported a cluster of silver rings on his little round left ear, pointed it out for her. Like the stars, it never seemed to move, so she didn't have any trouble finding it after that.

Boris claimed the *Manta Ray* was on a course that would lead them past Mars, but it was keeping complete radio silence. So, there were no transmissions to pick apart, no clues to figure out where the final destination of their trip might be.

Kipper stared at that dot among dots in the window, wondering where it was going and what would happen when it got there. What kind of conflict would occur between these two otter ships when the cats chasing each other on them caught up with each other? When she tired of her imaginings about a ship she could barely see, Kipper would find her way inward, back to the galley. Every day she swam less awkwardly but still uncertainly through the oxo-agua.

Emily gave her little tasks to make her feel busy while they "talked." Kipper was sure Emily could have got by without her. In fact, she suspected that her presence in the kitchen merely slowed Emily down. However, the otters still got their meals, and Kipper enjoyed learning about octopus cuisine. It was a very different animal from cat, dog, or otter cuisine. And, apparently, that's why Emily was onboard. The otters needed someone who knew how to cook on their very unusual ship.

Liquid atmosphere isn't fire friendly. Even heating coils are dangerous, since their heat doesn't stay contained. It leaks out, cooking the chef along with her creations. Thus, Emily's signature dishes were mostly raw. A few involved a pressure cooker, but, by and large, Emily prepared exquisite meals made almost entirely from raw or cured fish, shellfish, and various seaweeds. Kipper was skeptical of the kelp and algae based products at first, but Emily used them to perfection as skins and glues for the delectable mashes of cured fish and chunks of savory raw fish.

"You're getting better. You'd make a good octopus," Emily signed one day after watching Kipper deftly handle the chopping of a long roll of wrapped, cured salmon. Kipper had impressed Emily by flipping each chopped segment with a flick of the knife so that they floated out of her way. She was using the semi-weightlessness of the water to her advantage. Something that came automatically to an octopus. And seemingly so to otters. But not to a cat, and Emily knew that.

"Thanks," Kipper signed back, barely restraining her impulse to open her mouth and try to speak. She still hated being underwater. *Oxo-agua.* Whatever. She figured she always would. "But, you know it's not true," she signed. "I'd be a terrible octopus."

Kipper watched Emily for a response, but her tentacles were all busy arranging the food they'd just finished preparing for the hungry otters who would soon come devour it. And her expression continued to be inscrutable. Kipper simply didn't know how to read a face that was only eyes and the expanse of skin between them. Certainly, Emily had expressions. The skin between and around her yellow eyes crinkled in terribly expressive ways, but Kipper had no idea what those different expressions meant.

Kipper went back to chopping, and when she finished she put the knife away, arranging it carefully among the other knives stored on the magnetic knife block. She glanced back to Emily and saw that the octopus chef's yellow eyes were waiting to catch hers. "You'd make as good an octopus as me," Emily signed.

Kipper begged to differ, but she was so boggled by Emily's statement that she couldn't think of any of the otter signs she would need to say so. She could only think of the octopus signs, and her mammalian limbs couldn't make those. Feeling frustrated with her poor grasp of the only language available to her, Kipper settled for signing the first thing she could work out the otterly gestures for, "Is that why you're here? You don't make a good octopus?"

Emily fluttered her tentacles about in a gesture that Kipper recognized had no Swimmer's Sign meaning. It was an expression of emotion, but, unlike Emily's "facial" expressions, Kipper had developed something of an interpretation of it. It made her think of a cat or a dog sputtering. Except, since Emily spoke with her arms, she sputtered with them too. Finally, her tentacles settled down and she signed, "There isn't much room for women under the ocean."

Kipper waited, and, after a little more tentacle fluttering, Emily continued. "Once we lay our eggs, and safeguard them, most octopus women waste away and die."

"Why?" Kipper signed.

Emily flipped all her forward tentacles sucker-side up. Kipper interpreted the gesture as a shrug, since it also had no correlation in Swimmer's Sign. Though, she wasn't sure.

"Nothing left to live for?" Emily signed. "Too much effort spent on the eggs to recover from? I don't know." Here, the shrug again. "I didn't. Some don't. The men don't know what to do with us. We don't get treated the same as the mothers."

"You mean you don't get treated the same as the ones that *aren't* mothers?"

"No..."

"But, if you've laid your eggs, and they haven't..." Kipper signed.

More tentacular fluttering. "They have eggs in them. They can bear children. I am spent." A pause, and then, the shrug. "The otters don't mind."

Kipper couldn't help thinking (though, she could easily help saying since signing was still so difficult for her): "But, obviously, you do."

All the time Emily had spent signing to Kipper about the architecture of octopus buildings and the basics of octopus cuisine, the state of the art in octopus technology (they were on the verge of their own space program, only a few decades behind the otters)—none of it had really communicated to Kipper how the octopi lived.

They were so different physically... And, yet, Kipper wasn't prepared to disagree on such a fundamental concept as the meaning of motherhood. Even though she knew that octopi didn't raise their children like cats, dogs, and otters do... Even though she knew an octopus laid thousands, hundreds of thousands of eggs... Still, Kipper couldn't help trying to mold life in their society into a shape she was more familiar with.

Kipper was still wrestling with the idea, and Emily was still wrestling with the mesh baskets holding the coming lunchtime's scrumptious morsels, when Trugger rushed in. Actually, Kipper couldn't tell that Trugger was particularly rushing, because compared to her slow paddling all the otters moved ungodly fast.

He was swimming along the ceiling, his body undulating and twisting, webbed paws paddling to steer. A faded-purple and brown blur, seemingly at one with the currents and eddies in the oxo-agua. The spikes in his fur had been flattened out by the oxo-agua as soon as the *Jolly Barracuda* changed atmospheres, but the purple, though growing paler, was still there.

As he arrived in the kitchen, Trugger swooped downward, looping around in a loop-de-loop (an unnecessarily showy move if you asked Kipper), and finally halted at about the middle of the room. In all dimensions. His eyes went straight to the baskets of lunch in Emily's tentacles, but then he shook his head as if to refocus his attention and looked to Kipper. She was already watching him, so he started signing right away:

"The Doppler's shifted!" His paw motions were fast and exaggerated. They would have been hard to decipher under the best conditions, and Kipper's inexperience with Swimmer's Sign certainly didn't constitute the best conditions.

He repeated himself, signing more slowly and carefully: "The *Doppler* has shifted."

He looked very proud of his exclamation, but Kipper was neither familiar with the Swimmer's Sign for "Doppler" nor the concept of the Doppler effect. So, his care in signing didn't help her, and all she could manage in way of a response was, "What?"

Trugger did a somersault of giddiness or impatience in the water above her and then repeated himself. "The Doppler's shifted!"

Kipper frowned and signed, "What does that mean?" The signs came easier to her talking to Trugger. Since he was using otter signs and she was too, she was effectively working with only one new language where talking to Emily required two.

Trugger treaded through the oxo-agua, lowering himself to right in front of Kipper. He put his paws out, steady, before beginning to sign again. The equivalent of a deep breath. "The *Manta Ray* is slowing down. The Captain thinks we're stopping at Mars."

If Kipper had been standing on a normal spaceship, in a normal atmosphere, she would have lost her balance and lurched forward at the heart-stopping news: *finally, something was happening*. Instead, she floated placidly in the oxo-agua, her inner-turmoil utterly unexpressed in her outward posture. After a few moments—not enough to absorb the news, but enough to steady herself slightly—she signed with shaking paws, "What's on Mars?"

"Nothing, as far as we know," Trugger signed. "If otters wanted to live on planets, we'd still be on Earth. So... It might be exactly what you're looking for."

Kipper wasn't sure she needed to see those words, needed to know that anyone else was thinking the thought she held so dear that she could barely think it herself. "All right, then," she mouthed, knowing the words wouldn't carry, but unable to keep from speaking to herself. She looked about her, saw that the knives and other kitchen tools she'd been using were safely in order, and then kicked off from the floor. She paddled her tiny, unwebbed paws, treading through the oxo-agua, but as she passed Trugger he put out a spread, webbed paw and, placing it on her shoulder, stopped her.

"Where you going?" he signed with the free paw. It happened to be a one-handed phrase.

Kipper scowled at him for impeding her progress and signed with claws out, catching at his fur as her paws flew past his chest, "The bridge. I need to see what's happening."

"It's almost lunchtime," Trugger signed. He could see her bafflement, so he continued, "Nothing will happen again for hours now. It will take a day or two for the *Manta Ray* to decelerate."

In her impatience, Kipper signed as fast as her paws and memory let her: "I thought the whole point of the oxo-agua was to let the ship stop fast." The oxo-agua, whipped into a frenzy by her flying paws, kept whirling around them when they stopped.

"We can stop fast," Trugger signed. "The *Manta Ray* can't. And, even though it looks like they're slowing down for Mars, we won't be sure until they get closer. Or send a transmission. So, there's no point in us shooting past them and screeching to a stop. Sure, we'd arrive at Mars sooner, but that won't be any good if they never arrive at all."

Kipper started to object, but Trugger anticipated her objection and cut her off. Her paws slowed to a halt while his explained, "They could be slowing down for a tune-up. Or," he added, "to make a course readjustment."

Kipper flicked her ears and moved her jaws as if to speak, but her paws stayed still.

"There's nothing to do now," he signed. "Except lunch."

Emily had been watching their interchange, and when she saw Trugger's gaze move back to the basket of delectables held in her sinewy, suckery arms, she lifted the wire mesh contraption and waved it. The delectables tumbled about inside, and Trugger signed, "Yum."

Trugger stayed around to help Emily and Kipper set up the galley for lunch. The mesh baskets latched onto the tabletops where lunching otters could pull back a hinged door to reach in after the delectables. The hinged door sprung back into place, keeping the food inside, once it was let go. This way Emily's carefully prepared food didn't end up floating messily about the mess hall. Less clean-up; less wasted food.

Of course, the otters wouldn't have had to sit at the tables to eat, but it preserved some of the normality of life that got lost in deep space for weeks and weeks at a time. And, quite simply, it was more orderly.

Very little of the conversation at lunch was about the *Manta Ray's* change in acceleration. So, Kipper couldn't keep up with it. All she could think about was the *Manta Ray*. And Mars.

An empty red planet. Desolate, dry. She had to admit that dry sounded appealing, especially to a cat who'd been thoroughly soaked, inside and out, for far too long. But, even if she didn't like oxo-agua, a cat has to breathe. And Mars didn't provide much in the way of atmosphere. If there were cats on Mars, they'd have a hell of a time financing their oxygen. Kipper hadn't even been able to legitimately afford getting into space. How could cats like her ever expect to build some dream colony on Mars?

That afternoon, Kipper hung around the back of the bridge instead of studying her Swimmer's Sign and helping Emily prepare dinner. The bridge was mostly quiet—metaphorically speaking. (Literally, of course, it was almost entirely quiet; all noise dampened by the oxo-agua atmosphere except a soft, ever-present creaking of the ship that sounded like a distant whale song.) Otters manned the various stations, monitoring the condition of the *Jolly Barracuda* and tracking the progress of the *Manta Ray*.

When Captain Cod turned to Kipper and offered an encouraging smile, she signed, "What's the point of the oxo-agua if we have to follow a normal atmosphere spaceship just as if we were in a normal atmosphere ourselves?"

She'd spent fifteen minutes working out the signs for such a complicated sentence and another half hour waiting for the captain to look at her. She didn't want to risk being seen as an annoyance on the bridge, so she didn't disturb him to get his attention. But, surely, it was reasonable to sign a question while he was already looking.

All the captain signed back was, "You'll see." Then he turned back to his work, like the other otters on the bridge.

Chapter 14

The evening and night both passed slowly. At dinner, the crew of the *Jolly Barracuda* talked about the various mining expeditions or scientific surveys of Mars they'd either been on or known members of. As far as Kipper could tell, the only otter onboard to have actually put paw to soil on Mars was Boris. Well, space-suited paw. Nonetheless, he was clearly proud of the distinction and told the story of his visit in great detail. The other otters seemed impressed. Kipper wanted to slug him.

He'd been on a scouting mission to find a good location for a resort of sorts. An otter get-away, nestled among the rugged, red hills of Mars. The moral of his story? "Nowhere on Mars is worth two shakes of a jaybird's tail." He grinned as he signed it, and then he leaned back complacently and fiddled with his row of silver earrings.

It made Kipper furious. She wanted to sign back, "Maybe for otters!" But, she didn't know yet that cats felt any differently... She just hoped they did.

She excused herself and swam to her favorite window to watch the *Manta Ray*, imperceptibly decelerating as it approached the red ball of Mars. Yes, she could make out Mars now. It was no longer lost in the wash of identical stars. In fact, the more tired she got, the more convinced she was that she could see it growing as the *Jolly Barracuda* grew nearer. She sent herself to the barracks and to bed before she tried to convince herself that she could see cats joyously dancing on the distant red surface.

The dancing cats, however, found her in her bed. In Kipper's dreams, the *Jolly Barracuda* landed on Mars to find Petra already there, dancing with Violet and every cat Kipper had ever seen abused or put down by a dog in her life. Petra, Violet and all the other cats were dancing, unsheltered, on the harsh surface of Mars. Even Alistair and Sahalie were there, waltzing on the red rocks.

Violet saw her and left the others dancing to come toward Kipper. She came in leaps and bounds across the dusty, red rocks. As she came closer, Kipper could see that her face and mouth were transformed—surreally melded to a breathing apparatus. Kipper felt her own face similarly transformed, and the thin Mars air felt thick in her throat and lungs because of it. The surface of Mars was no different from oxo-agua. "How can you breathe this?" she tried to ask Violet, but her mouth was a contraption of rubber pipes and tubes. The sound wouldn't emerge, and the harder Kipper tried to scream her question the more frustrated she became.

Finally, Kipper awoke screaming. Except, like in her dream, no sound came from her mouth, except for an impossibly quiet high-pitched whine. She coughed and choked, gasping for air and only finding oxo-agua. She'd woken like this most of her nights on the *Jolly Barracuda*. But, the spookiness of seeing Violet and her littermates with those gas-mask faces still clung around her, making the morning ritual of hyperventilation worse.

Eventually, she calmed herself and slowed her breathing, accepting the thick, liquid atmosphere as the only one available to her. She looked around the barracks and saw many otters sleeping in their bunks. It was still early. And none of them had been disturbed by her nearly silent fit. In a normal atmosphere, her screams would have woken them all.

In a normal atmosphere, she wouldn't have awoken screaming.

Also, in a normal atmosphere, she could have risen from bed and washed her night terrors away with a relaxing shower. Though cats don't like living in water, they can appreciate it. Especially when it's moving. And in limited, controllable quantities.

On the *Jolly Barracuda*, however, Kipper had to settle for grabbing one of the otters' chemical brushes and giving her fur a thorough brushing.

The rough bristles felt good, but she had trouble feeling truly clean in a liquid atmosphere. Trugger had assured her that the oxo-agua was constantly being filtered and treated. Kept as pure as any air. But, no matter how he reassured her, Kipper couldn't reconcile herself to breathing the same substance she was swimming in.

She shuddered, finished brushing her fur, dressed in the shorts and vest that had become her uniform onboard, and headed to the bridge.

She tried to dawdle on the way, because she knew there wouldn't be anything happening. She knew it. But she hoped otherwise.

Her dawdling brought her past the galley where she could see Emily clinging to the ceiling, still asleep. Her suckers stuck tight above her and her tentacles coiled about in twisty patterns. Her mantle, the round bulk of her body, rose and fell in the center of her twisty arms. The fine tips of her curled tentacles—*they were so thin at their tips!*—quivered in the disturbance of the oxo-agua blowing through her siphon, the tube organ she breathed through. She would awake and begin preparing breakfast soon. She was always deep at work when Kipper arrived to help her. Except this morning. Such a curse to be unable to sleep... And especially when one is waiting.

Kipper dog-paddled on to her window, where she made herself watch Mars, the *Manta Ray*, and the plethora of surrounding stars as long as she could stand it. Then, when she could take no more, she finished her swim to the bridge.

Boris and Jenny were the only otters there. Kipper was still sore at Boris, so she paddled over to the right side of the bridge, near Jenny. The turbulence in the oxo-agua from Kipper's swimming rustled Jenny's fur, and she looked up. Noticing Kipper, Jenny smiled and signed, "Up early."

Kipper nodded and settled in to watch. Since the bridge was mostly empty this early, there were free computer stations. Kipper claimed the one two down from Jenny and worked on studying her Swimmer's Sign. She might as well stay useful and try to keep her mind off of Mars and the *Manta Ray* while waiting.

Kipper occupied her time by practicing the signs for lyrics to a pop puppy band song she liked. It was a good way to help herself remember the signs, and puppy bands do have *some* good songs.

That's what she told herself, anyway. Besides, a cat lyricist wrote the song, not the puppy band members. Just in case Boris and Jenny didn't understand that, Kipper kept her body angled away from them. That way, they couldn't read her signed singing.

Kipper could sign her way smoothly through the chorus and was working on translating the second verse when the *Jolly Barracuda* detected a transmission from the *Manta Ray* to Mars. Kipper found out when Jenny, deftly as an otter in water, swam over to her and tapped her on the shoulder. Kipper jumped and the momentum started her drifting out of her seat.

"I'm about to go wake the captain," Jenny signed, "but, I thought you'd want to know right away."

Kipper was still worrying about whether Jenny had seen any of her paw-singing, but what Jenny signed next completely wiped that concern from Kipper's mind.

"The *Manta Ray* sent a short message to Mars just now. It was a simple voice transmission: 'We have another new settler for you.'"

There's no other way to interpret that, is there? Kipper asked herself. She wanted to ask Jenny, but her heart was racing too fast and her thoughts floating too high to speak in sign. So, instead, she floated dumbstruck, an inch off of her chair, as Jenny smiled and turned tail to swim away. The thick brown otter tail swished rhythmically as Jenny jetted toward the back of the bridge. Kipper watched until Jenny rounded the corner into the starboard corridor and disappeared from sight.

Then, Kipper pushed a paw down and launched herself into her own swim across the bridge. Except, she swam toward the front of the bridge where she paddled awkwardly from monitor to monitor, looking for information about the *Manta Ray*, or the intercepted message, or Mars. She learned nothing, but she kept trying to scry out any meaning from those cryptic computer screens until Jenny returned with Captain Cod. The two of them had apparently stopped to gather several more bridge officers along the way, because Kipper suddenly found herself on a fully manned bridge.

Otters zipped from one post to another, swimming like Kipper never could. She didn't have the body for it. Swimmer's Sign filled the room, paws flapping and gesticulating as each officer turned to report to Captain Cod. The captain floated calmly in the center, apparently following all their rapidly signed reports. Kipper didn't know how he could keep up—"listening" to every otter "talking" at once.

But, apparently, he did, and before Kipper could accustom herself to the flurry it all died down. Each otter officer serenely, diligently focused on his own post. Captain Cod turned to Kipper and signed, "Now you'll see what the oxo-agua can do."

Lights in the seam between the walls and ceiling began flashing—they danced from red through orange, yellow, and the rest of the rainbow, all the way back to red. A buzz jolted through Kipper's entire body. It jolted twice more, and then Kipper found herself being forcibly moved to the back of the bridge and helped into a chair. Jenny, the otter helping her, signed "That was the alarm system, so everyone knows we're about to hit high acceleration. Since you're not used to it, I thought it'd be better if you sat down."

Kipper nodded dumbly. She found her manners right as Jenny turned to swim back to her post, signing too late for Jenny to read it, "Thank you."

From her new, secure, and seated position Kipper could see all the bridge officers' paw signs whenever they "spoke" to Captain Cod. She couldn't follow all of it, but it kept her abreast of the ship's motions. Albeit, mostly after they happened, for she found it easier to decipher their signed statements with the added clues she received from feeling the ships' goings-on herself.

As she understood it, the *Jolly Barracuda* was accelerating at a much higher rate than the *Manta Ray* could handle. Of course, the *hull* of either ship would be fine with even more acceleration—but, the *Jolly Barracuda's* unorthodox oxo-agua atmosphere was necessary to cushion and protect the bodies of the ship's *passengers*. Instead of receiving the entire acceleration as an increased gravity, pushing downward on them all, they felt an increased water pressure, pushing inward on every part of their bodies. Too much acceleration would still crush them; but, they could handle a great deal more acceleration than the *Manta Ray's* inhabitants could.

Thus, they could arrive at Mars much sooner.

From Kipper's purely sensational perspective, she lost the

feeling of weightlessness she'd known during her time on the *Jolly Barracuda*. Instead, she could feel herself being pushed downward in her chair, and she could feel the oxo-agua hugging her closer. This feeling rose until she could almost stand it no more. Her breathing was labored. (Not that breathing had ever been a joy in the oxo-agua atmosphere.) Her head felt light, and her chest felt heavy. Then, finally, she felt the gravity lessening. When it dropped back to where she felt weightless, she saw the stars spin in the windows around the bridge.

The bridge was set at the top, or nose, of the ship, with all the other living areas clustered not far beneath it. The bottom, tail-end, of the ship hosted all the cargo bays. That way, the greatest water pressure during maneuvers like these would only squeeze on inanimate boxes. The crew was, essentially, just under the surface of the miniature ocean contained inside the *Jolly Barracuda*. The cargo bays were at the ocean's depths.

The stars spun, Kipper decoded from the signage around her, because the ship had spun around to begin decelerating. That way, the live occupants were all still at the top of the ship, relative to the "gravity" that the ship's acceleration would make them feel.

And Kipper felt it. She clenched her teeth, not enjoying the feeling of being miles under the ocean one bit.

But, when it stopped, she looked out the bridge windows and saw Mars, larger than life, hanging before them. In fact, she couldn't really see Mars, per se—only part of it. Just the one horizon in front of them.

"Now tell me that you think oxo-agua is pointless," the captain signed to her, but Kipper's eyes were too full of the sight before her to understand him. The small red dot had grown in mere minutes to fill an entire sky.

Captain Cod understood and left Kipper to her Mars-gazing while himself returning to commanding the ship.

Chapter 15

Beating the *Manta Ray* to Mars was only the first step of Captain Cod's rapidly unfolding plan. The next stage involved doctoring the message they'd intercepted from the *Manta Ray*. They ran the voice through a simulator and used the simulation program to generate a new message. The new message said, "*Approaching Mars orbit.*"

Sure enough, within a few minutes, a signal was broadcast from the ground in response.

Kipper was still in her chair, in the back, when the response arrived. Trugger had made his way to the bridge and was keeping her company, pestering her with small talk questions and unnecessary information about the jump they'd just made past the *Manta Ray*. Kipper appreciated his effort to distract her, but it wasn't working very well.

"Kipper?" Captain Cod signed, after Jenny showed him the message from Mars. "We have a message from the planet." He and Jenny both beckoned Kipper over. She rose from her chair and began the awkward treading of water toward Jenny's post. Trugger swam slowly beside her, matching her pace. She felt like a cripple.

The weeks swimming and breathing a liquid, the uncertainty of her voyage and what had happened to Petra; being cut off from Alistair, Trudith, and everything else at home... It was all adding up. *Homesickness.* There was a feeling she never expected to experience for the dog-infested world she was born on. It didn't last long.

The words on Jenny's screen made it all—*everything*—worthwhile:

"We welcome your passenger to Siamhalla."

Trugger hugged her, and she could see over his shoulder, still squeezed into his hug, that all the other otters on the bridge were grinning at her. When Trugger finished trying to squeeze the oxo-agua out of her lungs, he pushed her far enough away to sign, "Now that's the name of a Cat Havana if I ever saw one."

"No kidding," Jenny signed.

Captain Cod put one paw on her shoulder and signed with the other one, "Congratulations." The rest of the bridge broke into a silent round of applause. Their paws clapped but the sound was absorbed before it could reach her ears.

Before they stopped, Jenny received another message. She signed so to the captain, and he signed for everyone to get back to work.

Kipper looked over Jenny's shoulder and saw that the second message read, "Open audio/visual contact?"

Her heart leapt to her throat, and she wanted to pour all her feelings out in words to the cats that must be waiting for her on Mars...

But the oxo-agua in her mouth strangled the breath of her voice out. Only a pathetic gurgling emanated. "How can we talk to them in this?" she signed, frantic with her desire to commune with cats instead of otters and dogs again. "They won't know Swimmer's Sign!" Her paws were emphatic, conveying every bit of her frustration and anger.

"Don't worry," Captain Cod signed. "Their transmissions showed us where they are. We'll fly down first, drain the oxo-agua, and then, when we're ready, we'll answer them."

"Won't they be suspicious?" Kipper signed.

"Why should they be?" Captain Cod asked. "There's no reason for a ship to be here except to find them. And no otter I've ever talked to has ever heard of a place called..." his signing faltered for a moment, since there wasn't a sign yet for Siamhalla. He ended up pointing at the message on the monitor, and Jenny helpfully spelled S-I-A-M-H-A-L-L-A out for him in alphabet signs.

Then, Jenny added, "This place is the best kept secret in the solar system."

"Until now. And, trust me," Captain Cod confidently signed,

"they won't see *us* coming."

Kipper almost smiled at that. She certainly flicked her ears in amusement. She had to admit that it would be hard for anyone to see the *Jolly Barracuda* coming. It takes a particularly quirky and off-kilter group of otters to jump at the chance to escort a broke alley cat across space on her wild goose chase. But, then, the Jolly Barracudas liked their bird metaphors. Singing lark, wild goose—it was all the same to them.

Trugger touched her elbow, and when she turned to look at him, he added with his paws, "Besides, we're just bringing them one of their own. One more cat to *Cat Havana.*"

Now Kipper did smile, her eyes warm with the look.

"Come on," Trugger signed, "let's get you ready for your journey to Mecca. We don't need to hang around waiting on the bridge anymore."

The captain agreed with Trugger, assuring her in sign that, "We'll get you into your Cat Havana. You just go and look forward to it."

Trugger marshaled her off the bridge and toward the galley for a bite of breakfast. Kipper knew she was being gotten out of the way, but she was happy to let it happen. *She was going to see Siambhalla soon.* She moved as in a daze, and, added to her normally slow rate of swimming, that meant she was barely moving at all. Literally floating.

When they finally arrived, Emily had breakfast dumplings all ready and no one to eat them. Everyone else was busy beginning the ship's landing. So, the three of them—cat, otter, and octopus—sat and ate.

Emily was excited to learn about the latest development: *Siambhalla.* The simple word rang with triumph, happiness, and mystery for Kipper. Even though she had yet to hear it pronounced—only read or signed—she could hear it in her mind; imagine it in her ears. *Music.* Sheer music.

Kipper let Trugger do most of the signing. She was too scared to believe her memories. Afraid that saying such outrageous things herself would make her and everyone else realize they must be untrue. Watching Trugger sign, deftly with his brown otter paws, though, was like reading the words to a fairy story. Meant to lull worried kittens off to sleep. She wished someone had read her his story when she was a kitten in the cattery. It would have given her something to strive for and dream about. Maybe she wouldn't have drifted uselessly from one temp job to the next if she hadn't thought the only alternative was a dead-end career like Alistair's or Petra's.

She hoped Trudith had gotten her brother out of jail by now, and found her sister. Maybe he really would be a government official by the time she got home. Unless... If Siamhalla was everything she hoped it was... Maybe she wouldn't be going home.

As they ate and Trugger signed, Kipper could feel the effects of the impending landing. The water pressure changed, and gravity grew and shifted; It was all the affect of the *Jolly Barracuda* entering a planetary atmosphere for the first time since Kipper had boarded.

Right as the three companions finished with their chewy, fishy, breakfast of dumplings, the alarm lights and buzzer went off again. Like they had back on the bridge. The ship was still for several minutes, having recently passed through a particularly bumpy phase. Trugger signed, "The buzzer means we've landed. The oxo-agua is going to drain now."

Emily waved her tentacles at her two companions, not in Swimmer's Sign—merely in a simple wave of goodbye, and swam back to the kitchen. She sealed herself behind plexiglass walls, returning to the cage she'd been in when Kipper had first seen her.

Kipper returned Emily's wave, saddened to see her friend caged like that, but the sadness couldn't live long. Self interest always wins in the end. Especially in a cat.

Soon (not nearly soon enough, nothing but *now* could be soon enough) Kipper wouldn't be breathing water anymore. And, with the ship landed, she was finally on the same planet as her dreamland for cats! She could have jumped for joy—except, she knew jumping would be easier once the oxo-agua drained, and the atmosphere was back to being gaseous again. (*A treat in and of itself: to breathe air again... to walk instead of swim...*)

So, she waited. Eagerly, impatiently.

The draining began with a kathunking, not so much a sound as a feeling in the floors. Then, looking up, Kipper could see a shine of silver appearing over the ceiling. The silver grew thicker, and she realized the silver was the air she would soon be (and longed to be) breathing. It descended slowly, unbearably slowly, at first. But, Kipper didn't swim up to it. She restrained herself, knowing she would just find herself flailing in the oxo-agua, thrashing, feeling like she was drowning in her attempt to escape the last few minutes of it. No, it was better to stay in her chair, accept the wait where she was already equilibrated.

As the layer of air above their heads gained width, it lost the silvered quality and grew into a green portal that stretched and distorted the world Kipper could see above her through it. Finally, just as the oxo-agua lowered to barely over her head, Kipper saw whirlpools, little tornadoes of air stretch down from the air ceiling into the drains below. Kipper closed her eyes, waiting for the air to touch the tips of her ears. Just waiting. Waiting.

Waiting.

And there it was: the tingly, strange feeling of the oxo-agua draining away, leaving her ear tips high and dry. Not really dry yet, but drier than they'd been in weeks.

Kipper kept her eyes closed and savored it until she could feel the air crowning her head. Then, unable to wait, she opened her eyes and stood up from her chair.

Oxo-agua dripped down her face and shoulders. She coughed the oxo-agua out of her lungs, lurching forward, curling herself around lungs that felt wrongly light and heavy. She felt Trugger grab her, support her, and pound her back, helping her hack the oxo-agua out of her lungs. Replacing it with wonderful air.

Except, the air didn't feel wonderful... It felt dry and scratchy, chafing a throat that had grown used to breathing horrid liquid... *Breathing liquid.* So wrong.

When she got her eyes open again (they also hurt in the now unfamiliar gaseous atmosphere), the view in front of them looked strangely... firm. Nothing wavered like it had; flowing with the feel of a mirage. She'd grown used to that. Without it, she found herself stumbling, and she didn't have the forgiving cushion of oxo-agua to catch her.

She splashed about, as pathetic as a kitten thrown in a pool by cruel, prankster puppies. Again, Trugger kept hold of her and helped her to stand until the oxo-agua got low enough to sit her back in the chair.

There, she panted and spat and heaved, finally calming and re-equilibrating to the atmosphere she'd looked forward to returning to for so long. She hadn't realized the transition would be so hard. Such a system shock.

"Hey," Trugger said.

Kipper's ears perked up, straight and forward. It was the first time she'd heard Trugger's voice, or any clear sound, in weeks. Kipper looked at him and smiled. "Hi," she said, feeling funny and shy. It was like they were introducing themselves for the first time all over again, like the last few weeks hadn't counted. They'd been in a different world. An underwater world. A world where cats don't belong.

Now it was time to be in a world where cats did belong.

"Are there showers?" Kipper asked. Her voice felt shaky from disuse, and her throat felt raspy. Air felt thin and harsh on all the exposed parts of her skin—her nose, mouth, and eyes.

"The ship isn't plumbed that way," Trugger said. He could see the betrayal in Kipper's eyes. "We don't spend enough time docked for it to make sense."

Kipper sighed and stood up awkwardly. Her limbs felt tired, automatically, in the new, less supportive atmosphere. "I guess another chemical brushing will have to do then." She was still gripping the arms of the chair, using them as a prop. She was thankful she didn't fall down when she gave them up. "There," she said. "I can still walk."

Trugger smiled. "The transition's hard. You've been swimming a long time. And you weren't built for it the way we were."

"No," she agreed. "I was built for this. Now, I'm gonna get myself back to the barracks, get this hideous *oxo-agua* out of my fur, and make myself as presentable as possible before I let any other cats see me."

"Fair enough," Trugger agreed, and, with some tactfully proffered help from him, that's exactly what Kipper did.

Kipper didn't know if they'd been waiting for her on the bridge, but it felt that way from the subtle change in postures and attitudes when she and Trugger arrived. She'd been glancing out all the windows as they walked through the ship—too nervous to really look, but too drawn by the lure of what might lay right outside not to. She hadn't seen anything that told her much about where they'd landed. Just red mountains, pale red sky, and the occasional metal-looking obstruction. Possibly the corner of a building or other structure.

"Where did we land?" she asked.

"The ground-controller of Siamhalla was kind enough to open the entry hatch to their elegant city-dome. So, we landed right inside." Captain Cod grinned a giant otter grin. Then, he came up and gave Kipper a giant otter hug, leaning his lanky body down over hers and wrapping his short arms around her shoulders. "Welcome to the inside of Siamhalla," he whispered before straightening back up.

There was brief applause and cheering from the other otters on the bridge. Trugger grabbed Kipper by the paw and squeezed. She squeezed back, affirming his silent congratulations, before he stepped away and joined the others in their noisy ones.

"Now," Captain Cod asked, "Are you ready to take a look at our new hosts?"

"*And let them take a look at us...*" Kipper whispered to herself. She dug her claws into the loose folds of her baggy otter trousers. Too baggy *and* too short. She felt all the otters looking at her, completely unaware of how foolish and self-conscious she felt in such obviously ill-fitting otter clothing. *They* weren't cats; they didn't know how clothes should fit her, or maybe they didn't care. Any cat would. Yet these knee-length otter trousers and almost knee-length otter vest, brand new from a fashionable boutique on Deep Sky Anchor were the best she had. The cats of Siamhalla would have to understand that.

Besides, she knew, whatever another cat thought of her clothing would be completely dwarfed by opinions on her fading faux-Mau fur job.

Deep breath. Dry air, whistling between her teeth. "Yes," she said, loud for all the bridge otters. "Let's see some cats."

"Great," Captain Cod said, putting his arm out, placing a paw on Kipper's shoulder and guiding her over to a station at the side of the bridge. Jenny scurried over and worked the switches, adjusted what looked like a microphone and video-feed.

An image popped up on the monitor between the mic and video feed: an empty box with a smaller box in the corner; Kipper and Captain Cod were in the smaller box. Kipper shuffled uncomfortably at the sight of her own image, and the image shuffled uncomfortably back. That wouldn't do. So, while Jenny signaled Siamhalla by text that the *Jolly Barracuda* was ready to talk to them, Kipper straightened herself out. She'd found the Cat Havana she'd been looking for—she put that pride in her posture and eyes. Then she looked ready. And not a moment too soon, for the larger box on the monitor jumped to life.

The new image was a stately Siamese man standing beside a pleasantly fluffed Birman woman. The Siamese was very handsome—broad shoulders, thin waist, elegantly tapered arms crossed over his chest. Kipper felt her ears burn hot at the tips, seeing both his and the Birman's stern expressions.

"We weren't expecting your ship," the Siamese said. He tilted his head forward; his eyes were piercing, but Kipper realized he was looking at the Captain, not her. "Our usual cargo ship is the *Manta Ray*. When you signaled, we assumed you were them."

"Yes," Captain Cod said. "Captain Larson and the *Manta Ray* are on their way,"—a brief pause and a huge grin—"but my ship is *faster*. And our guest was impatient to get here."

There were chuckles from some of the otters on the bridge. Kipper thought she could hear Trugger saying something about an "understatement." Then, Captain Cod threw a casual arm around Kipper's shoulder, urging her to step forward. As she did, she could see the Birman look at her and then up at the taller Siamese. His eyes narrowed as he looked at Kipper, and she could feel herself freeze, from the tips of her ears to the usually fidgety tip of her tail.

The glinting blue eyes, measuring her and judging her, softened. He said, "I'm Josh," gestured to the Birman beside him, "This is Elle. Welcome to your new home..." He trailed off with a clear question in his voice.

Kipper answered, "Kipper."

"Welcome home, Kipper," Elle said.

Josh added, "Come on out. We'll show you around." With a final, skeptical look at the clownish otter captain standing beside Kipper,

Josh reached forward and cut the video-feed.

There was silence on the bridge. Kipper wondered if the otters could tell how much Josh and Elle had disliked them. It made her nervous to look over at Captain Cod and catch his eye, but when she did, her question was answered.

He broke into a broad grin and said, "They seemed nice. I think I'd like doing business with them." He hadn't sensed their coldness toward him at all. "And, if they're working with Larson now, all we have to do is show them that our ship is better and," he looked around the bridge at all his subordinate otters, "our crew is a lot more personable. They seemed personable. Surely, they'd rather work with friendly, personable otters like us than Captain Larson's... *indifferent* crew." He rocked back on his heels, then forward on his toes. The bouncing motion traveled along his entire spine, adding up to a cheerful, endearing hop. "Yes, I think we've got a real chance here."

Kipper smiled weakly, her ears at half mast.

"Now, let's get out there," Captain Cod continued, "and let you take a good look at what you've come so far to find."

Kipper knew better than to point out that Josh hadn't invited the Captain. Just her. If none of the otters were cued enough into cat social cues to catch that subtlety... Well, Kipper didn't want to be the one to tell them. They'd find out soon enough. Or, maybe, if these Siamhallese were tactful enough, and the Jolly Barracudas were obtuse enough... Well, maybe they wouldn't have to find out at all.

Chapter 16

Boris was left in charge on the bridge, and Captain Cod asked Jenny to come along as a second pair of otterly eyes. If Josh and Elle hadn't seemed so cold toward Captain Cod, Kipper would have asked Trugger to join them too. But, if it got awkward, she didn't want to watch Trugger, the best friend she had among the otters, be treated cruelly. Or, perhaps worse, watch him watching these cats be cruel or cutting to his captain. He was so loyal; he would have to leap to Captain Cod's defense. She especially didn't want to see that.

So, when Trugger offered to walk with her, Captain Cod, and Jenny to the docking hatch, Kipper didn't invite him to accompany them any further. She just thanked him for the company that far.

"Remember everything," Trugger said. "We'll all want to hear about it."

When Kipper hesitated to promise, Trugger misinterpreted the pause and said, "I know you're coming back. All your clothes are still in the barracks."

Kipper smiled and dipped her ears a little. "Of course, I'll come back and tell you everything," she assured him.

She didn't explain that the few ill-fitting otter clothes stowed under her bunk in the barracks would hardly compel her to come back. She also didn't explain that her hesitation stemmed from wondering just how much a culture created entirely by and for cats would be understandable to otters.

"We'll all be waiting," Trugger said, bobbing in an otterly way as he backed down the corridor before turning and leaving her with the captain and Jenny.

The Captain was already standing at the docking hatch, working the panel beside it. Kipper glanced at the row of hanging, lifeless space-suit bodies, ignored behind a plexi-glass door. "No space suits?" she asked, nervously wondering whether there'd be any way to cram her long, cat limbs and (relatively) short, cat spine into an otter space suit.

"We're inside the Siamhalla dome already," Jenny said. "There's an atmosphere outside... See?" As Jenny spoke, Captain Cod finished with the control panel and stepped away. There was the sound of machinery moving and adjusting inside the wall. Then, the hatch doors parted.

Cool air rushed in, fluttering the baggy folds of Kipper's trousers. She'd thought the *Jolly Barracuda* air was dry after breathing liquid for a month, but it was nothing to Mars air. *Siamhalla* air. Kipper shivered. And only partly from the cold. Her fur, body over, was standing on end. She tried to calm herself so she wouldn't look like a fluffed-out, scaredy-cat when Josh and Elle and any other cats out there saw her.

It mostly worked. Through tight focus and steady breathing, she got the fur on her arms, face, and back to lay flat again. She could feel that her tail was still three sizes larger than usual, but she couldn't focus on that or the rest of her would fluff up again.

She'd just have to keep her broom-tail behind her, out of sight, until her jitters faded.

Captain Cod and Jenny, blissfully unaware of the last minute terrors striking Kipper, were already stepping cautiously out of the hatchway. They bobbed their heads, snaking their spines in the funniest otter way. "Come on, Kipper," Captain Cod called back to her, having taken the short hop onto actual Martian soil. "You've got to get out here and feel this Mars dust under your feet."

"It's warm," Jenny said. "Just like you'd imagine."

Despite her fears and excitement about Siamhalla, Kipper found herself completely distracted from any thoughts about other cats by the mere idea of touching paw to another planet. She ducked her head through the hatchway door and stepped down to join her otter friends on *Mars*.

The ground *was* warm. Dry, dusty, and solid under her paw pads. She flexed her claws and felt them scratch the Martian surface. She looked up and saw the Siamhalla dome curving overhead. Metal scaffolding and clear panes held them safely inside the dry air they were breathing. The sun glared harsher in a dusty sky. No clouds. Just pale sienna all across the overhead dome. Horizon to horizon.

Kipper continued marveling at the fact that she was standing on another planet—a planet other than Earth—until the snowy pale, muscled arm and midnight dark paw of Josh reached out to touch her own arm. She startled, her consciousness coming back down from the Martian sky to inhabit her body.

For the merest instant, she was embarrassed to return to the shoddily, growing out spots that covered her, but thoughts of her own body couldn't last long. She found herself standing beside the most handsome cat she'd ever seen. Perhaps that should have made her more embarrassed rather than less, but his eyes looked too deeply into her own to leave any room for it. There was no judgment there. Only welcome. Home. Could this be home? Kipper shifted her weight from one paw to the other, and while her eyes held his blue eyes steadily, she could feel her ears wandering in every which direction. So discomfited she was by his preternatural gaze...

"You brought nothing with you?" Josh asked, breaking the spell.

"Except otters, I see." There was a hiss under the dulcet tones of Elle's voice.

Josh broke his gaze with Kipper to look at her two otter companions. They were bobbing their heads about, getting the best view they could of Siamhalla from around their parked ship.

Josh's look was friendly at first, but that quickly faded. Kipper could see that his look was one of dismissal, and every moment he expected her escorts to leave. And he grew more surprised and irritated every moment they didn't. Kipper shifted her weight from one paw to the other. She wanted to apologize for Captain Cod and Jenny's rudeness... But they weren't being rude. All they'd done to offend Josh was in their mere presence.

"Thank you for the fine job you've done bringing one of our lost souls to us."

Kipper could have melted into a puddle at Josh's feet. Handsome *and* eloquent. Yet, she could hear the subtext, and she knew her otter companions couldn't. She was thankful that Josh had the tact and poise to handle his conflict with the otters subtly. Perhaps without even letting them know that there was conflict.

But what did she expect? She was back among cats again. And most cats could think circles around the otters socially. Cat social dynamics were ever so much more complicated.

"You can go now."

On the other paw, cats were still capable of the direct approach. Apparently, Josh didn't think her otter friends required tact, poise, and subtlety if they weren't perceptive enough to have already understood him.

"The captain was hoping for a tour," Kipper said.

Josh's ears meandered backward and forward again in confused displeasure.

Kipper pressed the captain's suit further. "They've come a long way." He and Jenny were staring about themselves, completely unaware of what was going on between them and the Siamhalla cats. They needed someone on their side who did know.

"I suppose they have hosted you for many weeks; we could host them for a few..."

Kipper could hear him struggling not to say *minutes*. However, he couldn't find a time frame he liked better, so he let the sentence trail off, unfinished.

"Let me show you around," Josh said to Kipper, but this time he managed to make it more expansive, including Jenny and Captain Cod. It looked like it pained him to do so. Jenny and Captain Cod clearly didn't notice. Well, Jenny might have—Kipper wasn't sure. But, Captain Cod was as oblivious as ever.

"Singing seagulls," Captain Cod exclaimed, "Let's get going then. I've got to see what kind of a place you cats have whipped up for yourselves here on this red space rock."

"Singing seagulls?" Josh asked.

"I didn't think seagulls could sing..." Elle added.

But Captain Cod had already begun wandering around to the other side of the *Jolly Barracuda*. Kipper decided to follow him, and, in doing so, she got her first good look at the outside of the spaceship she'd been living in since leaving the Deep Sky Anchor. It wasn't what she expected.

Instead of a sleek, gleaming outline, the *Jolly Barracuda* sported a bulky, bulbous silhouette. It looked like the kind of spaceship she expected to see—only dressed up in a lifejacket, with an inner tube around its waist, and air tanks on its back.

While Kipper stared at the strangeness of the ship she'd been riding, Jenny and their Siamhalla welcomers passed around her, trying to catch up with the straying Captain Cod. Kipper took a last look at the *Jolly Barracuda* before scurrying after the others.

"She's a beauty, isn't she?" the Captain asked once Kipper caught stride with him. "I saw you lingering back there, checking out the good ol' *Barracuda*."

"Uh... yeah..." Kipper lied. "I've never really seen a spaceship before. Up close. I guess they don't look much like they do in the movies. I should've known not to expect Otterwood movies to be accurate."

Captain Cod turned to her and gave Kipper a funny look. "Accurate? Most Otterwood flicks are filmed with real spaceships. I mean, they are filmed in space. What do you think they're using? Models? Do dogs film their chase scenes with model cars?" He paused not quite long enough for Kipper to answer. "No, they go around blowing up the real things. We blow up the real things."

Kipper looked back at the ungainly, metal object behind them. Before she could express her confusion, Jenny said, "The *Jolly Barracuda* looks more like other ships when she's flying. See those extra tanks?" Jenny indicated the bulky protrusions that looked like scuba gear to Kipper. "Those inflate to hold the oxo-agua atmosphere when we're not using it. They fold back in when we are."

Kipper tried to picture the ship with the extra oxo-agua tanks folded back in. Yes, that would look more like what she expected. Sleeker. Better.

"The oxo-agua isn't compressible like air—that's part of what makes it so cushioning. But, it means that it takes up a lot of extra space to store it."

"Oxo-agua?" Josh asked.

"It's a liquid, breathable atmosphere."

Elle snorted. "You've been breathing a liquid?" she asked Kipper, derision dripping from her voice.

"Hey, that liquid is what let us outrun the *Manta Ray.*"

Jenny's dropped chin let Kipper know that Jenny wished she could stuff the captain's words back in his mouth just as much as Kipper did. Josh and Elle looked at each other meaningfully before Josh asked the inevitable question: "Outrun the *Manta Ray?*"

At least the captain knew enough to keep his mouth shut now.

"Why were you racing the *Manta Ray?*" Elle hissed.

Though, some damage control wouldn't hurt...

Josh was still staring the captain in the eye, but Elle was eyeing Kipper like she was a stowaway rat. "Josh," she said, "I think we may be dealing with an imposter. How did you find out about us?" Her eyes on Kipper were like knives pinning her down. Kipper couldn't think to lie; her greatest fear, being discovered for a fake in the one place she most desperately wanted to belong, was coming true. Elle couldn't have broadcasted her disdainful thoughts more clearly.

"We outran the *Manta Ray* because we outrun every ship of a standard design," Jenny said. "That's why Kipper commissioned us. She didn't want to wait around with the cargo." Thank goodness for Jenny.

"That's right," the captain jumped in, finally catching the drift. "We hated to see a nice cat like Kipper stuck working with such foolhardy incompetents."

"Hmmph," Elle said. "We've never had any trouble with Captain Larson or the *Manta Ray.*"

"Yes, but they don't get your cats here as fast as we do. Do they?"

Josh looked like he wanted to deny it but couldn't. Elle simply looked like she wanted to claw Captain Cod's face.

"We'd like to work with you, and when you see how much longer it takes the *Manta Ray* to get here, I think you'll be interested in working with us too. Consider shuttling Kipper a free sample."

Josh had looked like he was starting to buy it, but with that last line Captain Cod's consistency was blown. "I thought you said she commissioned you."

"Ah..." the captain stuttered buying time, "ah... yeah... but, we turned down her offer. We thought buying your good will would be more valuable in the long run."

Elle looked skeptical, extremely skeptical, but Josh decided to jump past skepticism to dismissal. "Whatever," he said. Turning back to Kipper, he said "See that building over there?"

Kipper followed Josh's pointing paw to see a curved, clear, dome-topped building spiraled all around with sun-bathed balconies. Layers and layers of balconies, latticed with ladders connecting them. The bottom floor of the building was open, more a series of archways holding the building up above a large open space than an actual interior.

And the whole courtyard-like ground floor was flooded with sunlight streaming all the way down from the wavy, glass, roof dome. It made Kipper shudder with a pleasant warmth just looking at it.

"That's where I live," Josh said. "Fifth floor, Southern side. You can see the balcony." Josh pointed, but there were too many balconies on the fifth floor for Kipper to recognize his.

"I don't have a balcony," Elle said. "My apartment's a penthouse." Her tail swished braggingly.

"You don't say," Captain Cod jumped in. "Penthouse? What a penthouse needs is fine quality art decorating it. We've been dealing in the work of some artists from the asteroids..."

Elle tried to cut him off with a glare but ended up having to resort to saying, "I've already decorated."

"You can always redecorate," the captain added helpfully.

"I won't."

"Siamhalla has very strict rules about imports and exports," Josh said. "We're a pure culture. Everything here is—culturally speaking—one hundred percent feline."

"What do you mean?" Jenny asked.

Elle sneered, "We don't let otter or dog art be brought into our colony."

Kipper was still savoring the words *one hundred percent feline* when Jenny followed up with the question: "What about art by Earth cats?"

"Dog art," Elle said.

"What?" Kipper exclaimed. She was hurt. She wasn't an artist, in any sense, but if she were... Had Elle just called her a dog?

"Earth cats live in a dog culture," Josh said. "So, their artwork would be polluted by canine sensibilities. We don't want any of that here."

Suddenly Kipper felt like a baby thrown out with the bathwater. "Polluted?" she said. "By canine sensibilities?"

"Well, not you," Josh replied. "Anyone can see that you're *pure cat.*"

Kipper felt a little better. But not much. She enjoyed the vote of confidence, but she wasn't sure what inspired it. Besides, all Josh had done was say that she was different from all those other Earth cats out there.

They continued walking around the terraced building, and Josh pointed out the other buildings as they passed them. Kipper had grown quiet, continuing to contemplate the "impurity" of cats grown up around dogs. Or otters. For, as they walked through the crowds of cats—all pointed Siamese, fluffy Birmans, ruddy Abyssinians, and other fancy breeds—the otters were causing quite the stir.

Kittens, running wild among the other cats' feet, stopped to point and mew. It was believable—in fact, Kipper did believe that— these kittens had never seen an otter before. Not even in the movies.

Had they ever seen dogs? Or even heard of them?

It was one thing to want a place of her own, but, Kipper hadn't meant for that place to deny the existence of her former oppressors... Just to relieve those oppressors of their power.

Yet, as she wandered the streets and lingered in building entrances, Josh telling them all about each building they passed, Kipper couldn't help but be dazzled. Questions about the morality of complete isolation began to seem... so very far away. Perhaps that is in the nature of isolation. But, try as she might to be outraged for the cats who were missing all this because they hadn't gotten themselves out of Earth's grabby atmosphere, Kipper kept falling into the charm and elegance of a world made, run, and populated entirely by cats.

Pointed ears, swishing tails, mysterious smiles behind ethereal whiskers—these were her people. They stepped carefully and quietly, each paw sure of its footing before bearing weight. No puppies chasing frisbees carelessly, callously knocking over passersby. No gallumphing giants—like St. Bernards or Mastiffs—crowding the more rightly sized cats, treading upon them without even seeming to notice their presence.

Though, there was something eerie about it. Everywhere Kipper looked, all the cats were... cats. To an alley-tabby who grew up surrounded by the unwanted pressure of canines all around her, these cats felt almost disturbingly self-similar. No variety.

Of course, there *was* variety. White, orange, gray; stripes, marbles, spots... All combinations. In fact, loping along the other side of the street, she could see a lanky Eqyptian Mau, covered in fawn spots. The true mirror of what she merely pretended. Near him, there were several shorter, rounder Burmese gathered together. And, Elle had split off from the little tour group to talk with another fluffy Birman. (She looked quite relieved by the excuse to ditch what must have felt like a carnival troupe tromping through her hometown.) Then, up ahead, there was a whole crowd of warmly colored, red-furred Abyssinians. Actually, that was odd...

Kipper looked around again. Elle with another Birman; a crowd of Abyssinians; several Burmese... Why, all the cats she could see were either alone or walking with others of their breed. She couldn't see a single Siamese and Abyssinian together. No Birmans and Egyptian Maus... No, they were all mixed up together; only, not very mixed up at all.

Kipper was pulled away from her disturbing observation by the realization that Josh had asked her something. "I'm sorry," she said, "I was so caught up in looking around..."

"You missed what I said?" Josh asked.

Before he could repeat himself, Captain Cod jumped in, exclaiming excitedly, "This building is where you're going to live!"

Kipper's ears straightened, forward-pointing as they could be, and she looked at the building with widened eyes. "There's already a place for me?"

"Well, not a specific apartment," Josh said.

"But this is where the new cats live?"

"No," Josh said, "We don't artificially stratify our society like that. This is where the Egyptian Maus live."

"But I'm not Egyptian Mau."

Josh stuttered, completely dumbstruck by Kipper's absurd statement. Eventually, he managed to get out, "But your fur..." Then, finding more confidence, he added, "Of course you're a Mau. What would you have me believe you are?"

"A tabby."

Josh looked highly skeptical.

"Look at the roots," Kipper said, turning herself before him to show her shoulder fur. "My stripes are already coming back in."

"You... you dyed your fur? Why are you telling me?"

"You seriously couldn't tell?" Kipper had trouble believing it. Maury's fur job had been good... but not that good. "I guess you're not used to that here. It happens a lot at home." She caught herself, "On Earth, I mean." She didn't mention that it was only trashy, street cats who did it.

"Well, I guess there's not much call for it here," Josh said.

Kipper's ears flickered a little in confusion. Then she looked around and realized what he meant. She didn't know why it hadn't sunk in before. "There are only pure breeds here..." Kipper felt dizzy.

Before she could speak again, Josh looked around quickly then took her by the arm. He dragged her off of the street into a back alleyway. "How appropriate..." she said, her voice babbling and bleak. "The only alley cat in Siamhalla, forced into the only alley. Clearly, anywhere as perfect as Siamhalla shouldn't have alleyways. It probably sprang into existence just now. Just for me."

"Hush!" Josh admonished her, placing his strong but graceful, sable paw over her mouth. Even reeling from the shame, outrage, and confusion of finding herself to be the only non-pedigreed cat left in the world, Kipper wasn't immune to the electricity she felt coursing from those dark paws and into her. Josh must have felt it too. He backed away, practically trailing chains of sparks.

"What are you doing?" he said, once the charge in the air had returned to normal. "I can't un-hear what you just told me. And, believe me, I don't want to be covering for you."

Captain Cod and Jenny, who had been examining a bit of the architecture when Josh pulled Kipper away, came poking around the corner of the alley. "Ah, there you are!" Captain Cod said. But Jenny quickly hushed him when she caught the tone of the proceedings.

"You'll have a hard time pulling this off even if I do cover for you..." Josh was clearly thinking the dynamics of it through. "You'll need regular supplies of dye..."

"Oh, it's not just that," Kipper added, helpfully. "You think I can do this myself? I had this done by a professional."

"Is that what you want?" Josh looked aghast. "You took me into your confidence so you could train me to be your conspirator? Keep you in Mau fur... *jobs*, as long as you're here?"

Kipper squared her shoulders and ears, an angry gleam in her eye, before answering him. "It was never my intention to spend the rest of my life passing for a Mau."

"How do you intend to stay then?" Josh asked.

Kipper's shoulders slumped a little, and her ears meandered as she found herself turning inward to really consider his question.

Memories of Trudith, helping her escape Earth; the last few weeks with Emily and Trugger; the kindness of that dopey Golden Retriever receptionist at her last job; and even that mushy, nutty squirrel food on the Deep Sky Anchor... She re-traveled them all. Then she looked deep in her heart, where she expected to find Siamhalla, the cat utopia she'd sought for so long. But it wasn't there. She'd found utopia, and it wasn't for her.

Deep down, she found the home she'd been trying to escape for so long. The crazy home where cats had to fight for their rights, but at least they were free to be whatever kind of cats they wanted to be. Trashy, faux-Siamese—or fake tigers, even.

Or just comfortable in their own, unremarkable, tabby-cat fur.

"I guess I don't," she said. Even as she said the words they surprised her, "I don't plan on staying."

"Are you sure?" Josh asked. "There won't be any changing your mind on this. Once it gets out that you're..."

She could hear him choosing not to say "a common alley cat."

Instead, he went with, "...not really a Mau..." He hoped that was diplomatic enough. "Once that's out there, it's out there."

Kipper was flattered that he liked her enough to want her to stay. Though, even if she had truly been a purebred Egyptian Mau, welcomed on Siamhalla, there could never have been a romance between them. Siamese and Egyptian Mau? How ridiculous would that be? On Earth, not so ridiculous. But here... Kipper suspected it would be a scandal.

Nonetheless, infused with confidence by Josh's seeming willingness to stoop to subterfuge for her, she put out her paw and grasped on to his. "I'm sure. I'm glad I got to see what Siamhalla is like. And... in an odd way... I'm glad it's out here. But I can't live in hiding all my life."

"Maybe once you'd been accepted... Once everyone got to know you..." Josh couldn't even finish saying it. They both knew it was a lie. A world like this wouldn't forgive the crime of pretending to be something you're not just because it got used to you.

Josh suggested she stay a few days and take this chance to experience Siamhalla before leaving, but Kipper didn't think it was fair to keep the crew of the *Jolly Barracuda* cooped up at a port where they weren't welcome.

"At least, let me walk you back to your ship," Josh said. "I can tell you about New Persia."

Kipper's eyes grew wide. "Another place like this?"

"Yes."

"There's another cat utopia?" Captain Cod asked, jumping in.

"Not so utopian after all," Kipper said. "But, apparently *yes*." Then, to Josh, she said, "That's an offer I'll accept."

So, Josh walked them back to the *Jolly Barracuda*, telling Kipper all about another cat colony in a bubble, this one peopled entirely and only by pug-faced, fluffy-haired Persians. By the time Josh and Kipper parted ways, Josh had pressed her to promise to keep in touch. He claimed he wanted to know about the outside world, but Kipper strongly suspected he had a crush on her. In a world where every cat has a pedigree, the one alley cat is extremely exotic. Nonetheless, she found his crush more than gratifying, and she was sorry to say goodbye.

Chapter 17

Trugger was glad to hear upon Kipper's return that he didn't have to say goodbye. He gave Kipper a big bear hug. He'd given her hugs before, but they'd all been in an oxo-agua atmosphere which simply isn't the same. So, this was Kipper's first time really being engulfed by the soft but incredibly dense pelt of an otter. The warmth was there under oxo-agua, but none of the fuzziness, and *fuzzy* just doesn't feel the same when wet.

"I knew you were a space pirate at heart," Trugger told her.

"I thought you said you guys weren't pirates."

Trugger shrugged, sitting back on his bunk. "Only to our own. We don't like to bandy the word around too much with outsiders. But you're one of us now!"

"Not so fast," Kipper said. "Just because I'm not some purebred show-cat that doesn't mean I'm not still a cat."

"A water-cat if I ever knew one."

"I'm not sure you *can* know one. I'm not sure there is such a thing."

"So, what're you saying?" Trugger asked. "You're gonna jump ship at the next port we come to? Bum around otter space stations?"

"I dunno."

"Well, you can't go back to Earth. You've been telling us all about how badly the dogs treat you for months now."

Kipper felt the need to call Trugger on his exaggeration. "*Months* is a generous appraisal," she said.

"Weeks then." He looked a little hurt to have the time they'd known each other minimized like that. However, hurtful or not, Kipper had only been in otter space for the last few weeks of her life. She'd grown up on Earth. She hated it... but it was part of her.

"I don't know," she said.

Trugger smiled weakly, stood up, and then reached over to affectionately ruffle the fur on her head. "By the way," he said, "We called back to the communications hub. There was a message for you. I picked up the cost. Figured you'd want to view it when you got back to the ship—not pay for it and wait for the download."

"Thanks," Kipper said. "I'll pay you back later."

Trugger left her sitting dazedly on her bunk. He was still a working otter. Technically, Kipper was supposed to be a working cat on this ship. They just never had figured out a job for her other than studying swimmer's sign all day. She guessed she'd been in training. Captain Cod had chosen to invest the time and resources into her to bring her up to speed to become a full member of the crew.

But Kipper wasn't sure she wanted to be a full member of the crew. Living in oxo-agua hadn't turned out to be as bad as she expected it to be... But it wasn't her idea of a long-term living environment either. Really, all along, her plan had stopped at Cat Havana. She would get there, and suddenly everything would be okay.

Siamhalla hadn't turned out to be Cat Havana though. Not quite. Honestly, it was exactly what she should have expected from a world run by cats—judgmental and exclusive. At least dogs professed to be inclusive, even if there was a glass ceiling over cats in their world.

Kipper sighed. Maybe there was a secret squirrel colony somewhere she could join. That would surprise everyone. Especially the squirrels. Maybe they'd be so taken aback by a cat wanting to join them that she'd find herself elected their leader. Kipper, Empress of Squirreldom. It had a nice ring. Or, maybe she was losing her mind.

Kipper decided it was time to hear her message, so she walked down the hall to the little work room with one computer console. She keyed up the message, and, as she sat down, it began playing.

"Kipper, I don't know when you'll get this," Alistair said, small and pixelated on the computer screen, but still the friendly, orange-striped face of her brother. "That dog you sent, Trudith, sprang me from jail. I was... well..." Alistair sounded like he was going to explain how he'd landed in jail in the first place, but instead ended up grumbling, "*Stupid outdated catnip laws.*" He shook his head. "Those dog-pandering laws will be the first to go when I'm elected. You don't see rawhide busts, do you? Anyway, thanks for Trudith," Alistair said, getting back on track. "She's a real find. I thought she'd want a tip and then she'd be on her way, but she seemed to have it in mind that she was my new bodyguard. I couldn't have beaten her off of me with a stick." Alistair looked ponderous for a moment. "Though... I suppose I could have tried throwing one..."

Kipper laughed at Alistair's conjured image. "A scramball would be more likely," she said, even though she knew Alistair couldn't hear her. Who knew how long ago he'd sent this... She'd have to check if there was some way to find out.

"Anyway," Alistair continued, also shaking the image of Trudith chasing sticks from his head. "She's turned out to be more than a bodyguard. An advisor, I'd almost call her. See, I'm running for *senator* now. The ruckus about you and Pet disappearing... All the doubt and uncertainty about what happened to you and who made it happen... We've played it up big time." He put his paws out as if he was framing a newspaper headline: "*Concerned older brother, trying to find his missing sisters, and make the world a safer place in the process.*" He looked very pleased with himself. "There's a huge investigation underway. So, far they've turned up all this dirt on that cat Sahalie, who you worked for. She was doing some kind of embezzling, and sending all the money somewhere. Apparently it's this huge conspiracy."

Bigger than you think, Kipper thought. *Those funds are funding a whole planet.*

"Anyway, no one but Trudith and me knows what really happened to you and Petra. So, everyone's in an uproar. There's a chance for some real change down here." He paused, thoughtfully. So clearly pleased with himself. Kipper warmed all over seeing him. "The polls are looking good," he continued. "Real good. I have a chance of actually making a difference. And, if I win, I won't be some figurehead cat. I'm gonna give these dogs a run for their money."

Hopefully, Kipper thought, *he'd give the purebred cats a run for their money too.*

"Anyway, if you can, try to come home. I want you to be here when I get sworn into office." On screen, Alistair reached his paw forward. What was he doing? What the hell?! He was switching the vid-phone off. That was the end of his message?!?

"What happened to Petra!!!" Kipper screamed futilely at the screen. As if in response, the screen flickered back to life.

"Oh, I almost forgot to mention," Alistair said, his paw still on the vid-phone toggle. "Petra married that dog from your office. Lucky. She says she doesn't remember writing any note about going to Ecuador, and her place was such a mess because they were both stumbling around completely drunk while packing. They're keeping it quiet for now. At least until after the election."

This time the message really was over.

Kipper blinked at the blank screen.

Lucky? Brother-in-law? She thought those two hated each other.

Huh. She had a dog for a brother-in-law. What a world.

Kipper thought about Alistair's campaign and how it would be affected when Petra's marriage came out. People didn't talk about interspecies relationships much. Honestly, Kipper didn't know what to think herself.

The more her mind wandered over everything Alistair had told her, the more Kipper found herself wondering about Sahalie. As far as Kipper could figure, Sahalie, and maybe other cats like her, sat high up in dog companies, embezzling money for Siamhalla and helping shuttle purebreds off of Earth. But, what was in it for Sahalie?

She was only half Siamese. There'd be no more of a place for her on Siamhalla than for Kipper. And, yet, Sahalie would fight tooth and nail to get Violet to Siamhalla while keeping Kipper away. It was so... *catty.* Maybe that was the problem with Earth, not that dogs were holding cats down but that cats were holding *each other* down.

Kipper sighed and keyed off the monitor after checking the date stamp on Alistair's message. It was already several weeks old. She wondered how the campaign was going. She wondered whether Sahalie was in jail for the embezzling, and whether there was a new cat to replace her yet. A place like Siamhalla couldn't rely on only one source. There must be cats all over Earth sending them funds.

She wondered if Violet would like Siamhalla better than she had. At least she had the right fur coat for it.

Violet had been the phantom Kipper was chasing for so long... and now she was leaving their destination before Violet had even arrived. *Two larks flying past each other in the night.* Kipper was spending too much time around otters.

It was time to go home. And face up to the fact that her home was her home. And that home was Earth. Cats like Elle might not have a place for her, but dogs like Trudith did. And otters like Trugger.

How was it that Cat Utopia was the only place in the solar system that didn't have a place for a cat like her? Not even a bad one, trodden under paw. Maybe it was time for Siamhalla to come to light. Under the scrutiny of the rest of the solar system, they'd have to think long and hard about their policies. And, without money being funneled to them by cats like Sahalie, she suspected they might need to open their arms to a wider cross-section of cats and the money those cats could bring.

No, Kipper wasn't done with Siamhalla yet. But the next steps for her to take toward creating a true Cat Havana were back on Earth. Not out in space.

About the author

Mary E. Lowd grew up in a house with three cats. Her favorite past-time was pretending they could talk and writing stories about them. She started her first novel at the age of eleven; it bore a striking resemblance to Brian Jacques' *Redwall*, replete with little woodland animals eating feasts and battling each other with swords. Her next abandoned novel had more in common with *The Pride of Chanur* by C.J. Cherryh, featuring first contact with a race of space-faring feline aliens.

Ten years later, several important things happened: Mary married a man who loves dogs, and she switched to writing short stories. The latter taught her the discipline to actually finish her works of fiction. The former... Well, it introduced Mary (who had hitherto been strictly a cat-person) to the complex interplay of "dogs and cats living together—MASS HYSTERIA!" This novel was the inevitable conclusion.

These days, Mary lives in a house with five cats and three dogs (along with her husband and daughter). One of those dogs is Trudy, a fifty-pound half-lab, half-spaniel *muse*. Trudith is completely and utterly based on her. And, in addition to stealing every scene she graced in this novel, Trudith has claimed center-stage with Kipper in *Otters In Space 2: Jupiter, Deadly*, which will be available as soon as Mary can contrive to finish it.

If you can't wait that long for more Trudy-inspired fiction, then check out Mary's website (www.marylowd.com) where you can find links to many of her short stories and her bizarre lolcats-meet-space-opera webcomic *SPACE HOUNDS!*

CPSIA information can be obtained at www.ICGtesting.com
Printed in the USA
LVOW07s0522260813

349542LV00001B/6/P